RIMROCK TOWN

WILLIAM HEUMAN

SAGEBRUSH
Large Print Westerns

First published in the United States by Arcadia House

First Isis Edition
published 2019
by arrangement with
Golden West Literary Agency

A catalogue record for this book is available
from the British Library.

ISBN 978–1–78541–694–1 (pb)

Published by
F. A. Thorpe (Publishing)
Anstey, Leicestershire

Set by Words & Graphics Ltd.
Anstey, Leicestershire
Printed and bound in Great Britain by
T. J. International Ltd., Padstow, Cornwall

This book is printed on acid-free paper

To HAROLD B. WARD

CHAPTER
ONE

Harlan Craig had come into Rimrock that morning on the ten o'clock train, and he was ready to leave it one hour later. The town and the surrounding country had a depressing effect upon him. Even breathing seemed to be difficult.

When the wind blew from the west, where most of the copper smelters were located, a brown, stinking pall hung over the town. The smell of sulphur was always in the air, and the blighting smoke had killed all vegetation for miles around. There were no trees to be seen, no grass, only the brown, lifeless hills of Montana, and the big hill, the billion dollar hill, containing vast quantities of copper and silver, looming up behind the town, not high, but huge, long, almost flat on top, almost like a grave mound, Harlan thought.

"Get used to the smell," the barber had told him as he was being shaved in the shop near the railroad station. "Ain't so bad when you're used to it, mister."

It wasn't only the smell. It was the noise from hundreds of stamps which were reducing silver ore down in Hell Valley a half-mile away; it was the sight of hundreds and hundreds of pasty-faced miners with red-rimmed eyes, moving with full dinner pails toward the mine shafts on the hill, and other hundreds coming from the hill with empty pails to pause in the dozens of saloons along the main street before going on to their drab shacks at the edge of the town.

"Have to hear Garrison speak this afternoon," the barber had said. "He's gonna rip into the company again. Biggest man in these parts, Boyd Garrison."

Harlan had heard talk of Boyd Garrison on the coast where he'd been operating his stage line. Garrison was the gallant little David battling the giant Goliath, represented by the United Copper Company in Rimrock. Garrison was the man of the people, fighting the big trust company for the precious metal in the hill.

There was no train out of Rimrock until morning, and at two o'clock that afternoon Harlan came out of the Bluebell Saloon where he'd tried in vain to get the taste of sulphur out of his mouth with a glass of cool beer.

Already, the main street in front of the City Hall where Garrison was to speak was jammed with people, mostly miners, but some cattlemen, too, who'd come in from the surrounding countryside, drawn by the magnet which was Boyd Garrison.

Pausing out in front of the Bluebell, Harlan took a cigar from his vest pocket, and was feeling for a match in his pockets when a tall, lean, cavernous man standing next to him on the walk scratched a match into light on the telegraph pole and held it in front of the cigar.

"Obliged," Harlan said around the cigar.

2

"Name's Barnhouse," the tall man told him idly. "Fred Barnhouse. *Rimrock Miner* — newspaper."

Harlan nodded his head slightly, and then put one shoulder against the pole. He was as tall as Barnhouse, but heavier, bigger in every way, solid in the shoulders, with black hair and gray eyes.

"Harlan Craig," he said, and would have let it go at that. But Barnhouse was a newspaper man, and inquisitive.

"You're not a copper man," he said thoughtfully.

"Stage line," Harlan told him.

Barnhouse grimaced. "You're dead," he said. "Railroad's killed you."

Harlan smiled faintly. "I died hard," he murmured.

But he had died. In 1889 a spur of the U.P. had reached the north California country where he'd operated the line. For three years previous to that time he'd fought to keep it going, after inheriting the company from his father, but the railroad had killed him as he'd known it would sooner or later.

After paying off his debts, he'd pocketed the small sum left and bought a ticket for Rimrock, the booming mining town of southern Montana which seemed destined to eclipse even the turbulent Virginia City in Nevada. Copper was the chief source of Rimrock's wealth, however, with industry consuming millions and millions of pounds yearly.

Fred Barnhouse was saying cynically, "So you came to Rimrock to become a copper millionaire."

"Figured I'd see it." Harlan smiled. "I'll be on the morning train, west."

Barnhouse lifted his eyebrows. He had deep-set hazel eyes, and a wide mouth to go with the lean hatchet face.

"You don't want a million dollars?" he asked.

"Not if this smell has to go with it," Harlan told him. "Reckon I'll go back where a man can breathe clear air."

Barnhouse sighed faintly. "It is good to know," he murmured, "that there are a few men like that left in this world. Most of us will take the million and breathe the fumes."

"How many make a million," Harlan asked him, "in this town?"

"William Andrews of United Copper has made it fifty times over," Barnhouse stated. "Boyd Garrison came here three years ago with less than five thousand in his pockets, and he is worth his million today."

Harlan puffed on the cigar, watching the crowd out in the street. Already there were several thousand men here, with a sprinkling of women. The street had been roped off in both directions to accommodate the crowd. The stone steps of the courthouse where Garrison was to speak were black with people.

"What is the occasion?" Harlan asked.

"Election speech," Barnhouse explained. "Special election in this town tomorrow. Garrison is campaigning for Judge Otis Brynn."

He nodded toward the porch of a nearby hotel, and Harlan looked at the short, slight, gray-haired man in the black suit standing there, looking out across the heads of the crowd. Judge Brynn had silvery hair, but a

4

young face with ruddy cheeks. He stood with his small child's hands folded in front of him, a pensive expression on his face.

Harlan, however, was more interested in the girl with him, undoubtedly his daughter. She was slender, dark, of medium height. The weather was turning cool in Montana in late summer, and she was wearing a tight-fitting gray suit with a white collar, and a rather pert straw hat with a white ribbon.

Harlan looked at the girl, conscious of the fact that Barnhouse, the newspaper man, was watching him, and then he said easily:

"That the reason Garrison is campaigning for Judge Otis?"

Barnhouse's answer was slow in coming. "Partly," he said. "Garrison is supposedly engaged to Miss Julia Brynn, the judge's daughter. It is also good for his business to have a circuit judge on the bench who is not unfriendly."

Harlan considered that fact. It was widely known that there were mining lawsuits in Rimrock involving millions of dollars' worth of ore, and it was understandable that a man who was on the right side of a venal judge would come out with rich plums. However, Judge Otis Brynn looked like an honest man.

Harlan looked at him, and then at his daughter. Julia Brynn turned her head slightly and saw him looking at her, flushed slightly and turned away.

"Garrison coming out now," Barnhouse said. "You'll hear something."

Harlan was prepared to see a portly copper magnate emerge from the crowd on the steps of the courthouse, and he was surprised when a tall, trim man, devilishly handsome, moved up to the top step and held up both hands for silence.

Garrison could not have been older than himself, and he hadn't reached thirty yet. He had golden brown hair, and a wide, boyish grin on his face. His voice was strong and carried clearly out across the crowd, which became instantly silent as he spoke.

It was a political speech pure and simple, with Boyd Garrison bringing out the fine points of the candidate he supported and denouncing the opposition. The cheers didn't come, however, until he went to work on William Andrews and the United Copper Company, the big trust which, as Garrison put it, had a stranglehold on the town.

"They are trying to control the state legislature," Garrison roared. "They want control of the judiciary so that they can enforce the laws their paid hirelings enact. You men who work for the company know what I'm talking about. You're not men; you're slaves. You must buy your food and your clothing in the company store; you save your few pennies in the company bank; you read the company newspapers."

Harlan glanced at Fred Barnhouse, and Barnhouse shook his head slightly.

"Not the *Miner*," he said simply.

Boyd Garrison's voice carried clear and strong over the big crowd. He was not a man speaking; he was a god, and they listened to him as one. They cheered; they yelled; they growled in their throats.

Even Harlan, who knew nothing of the politics of this town, felt himself beginning to dislike William Andrews, the multi-millionaire who controlled United Copper.

"You live in company houses," Garrison boomed. "You pay the company rent. The company tells you what you will receive for wages, and if they wish to lower your wages to increase their dividends, they can do it, and there is nothing you can do to prevent them. Vote for the United Copper Company candidates tomorrow, and you'll live all of your lives under United Copper rule, and when you die they'll bury you in United Copper coffins."

A deep-throated roar came from the crowd, and Harlan heard Fred Barnhouse chuckle softly.

"He's better than usual." Barnhouse grinned.

"We need a man on the bench in Rimrock who will do his best to keep the company in line," Boyd Garrison was saying. "We present that man to you, a man of unimpeachable honesty."

Harlan was no longer listening to Garrison's speech, however. His eyes had moved out over the big crowd, which had nearly doubled since Garrison had started to speak. They jammed the blocked-off street. Every saloon-front was black with them. They were sitting on the roofs of porches. The usual small boys were clinging halfway up the telegraph poles along the street.

Turning his head slightly, Harlan looked back at the porch of the Bluebell Saloon out of which he'd just come, and it was then that he saw the long barrel of a six-gun coming over the top of the bat-wing doors. There was a man's hat and the upper part of his face showing above the doors. The muzzle of the gun was lined on Boyd Garrison across the road.

The saloon was empty, and the two bartenders who'd been inside were out on the porch, listening to Garrison's speech. Harlan saw them standing on either side of one of the porch pillars.

Harlan carried a short-barreled Smith & Wesson .44 in the holster under his coat, but there was no opportunity to use it. Several men stood between himself and the killer behind the bat-wing doors inside the saloon. He would have to shoot between these men to hit his target, and if one of them happened to move his body slightly the slug would hit him.

There was only one alternative, and he had to act quickly. Sliding away from the pole, with Fred Barnhouse watching him curiously, he moved back to the edge of the porch, out of sight of the man behind the doors. Then he vaulted up over the low porch railing, coming up behind the groups of men who were standing there listening to Garrison talk.

It was twenty feet to the bat-wing doors, and Harlan covered the distance in a half-dozen long strides. Just before his shoulder hit the door behind which the killer was standing, he had a glimpse of the gun barrel resting steadily on the rim of the door.

As he hit the door the gun roared, but the aim of the killer had been spoiled. The slug smashed into the roof of the porch, and the man behind the door staggered back inside.

Harlan had only a brief glimpse of him as he himself stumbled forward, off balance, plunging to the floor. The force of his charge had ripped one of the hinges loose from the right door, and it sagged toward the floor.

The killer darted toward the rear door of the saloon as Harlan ended up under a table nearby. He could only see that the man wore a black, flat-crowned hat and a black coat, and that he was of average height.

There were shouts outside after the shot, and men came running into the saloon. As Harlan picked himself from the floor, his left shoulder aching, he heard someone yelling:

"They tried to kill Mr. Garrison!"

"Reckon this feller stopped it," another man said. "You see him, mister?"

Harlan shook his head as he dusted himself off. "Went out the back door," he said briefly.

One of the bartenders said to him, "Drink on the house, mister. Anybody saves Garrison's life can empty my stock."

A man with a star on his vest pushed through the crowd, stopping in front of Harlan. He was short and stocky, with a heavy, solid jaw and pale blue eyes.

"McAfee," he said to Harlan, "Cole McAfee, town marshal. You see the man tried to shoot Mr. Garrison?"

Harlan shrugged. "Saw the gun barrel on the door here, and it seemed to be lined on Garrison across the street. When I hit the door he ran out the back way. I saw the back of his head."

Fred Barnhouse, the newspaper man, had come into the saloon and was standing with the crowd, staring at Harlan curiously.

McAfee was saying grimly, "A rotten business, gunning a man like that."

Harlan scarcely heard him. He was looking beyond the short lawman, through the doors to the porch, where the crowd had gathered. Judge Otis Brynn was in that crowd, and there was a peculiar expression in his mild blue eyes.

Harlan was shocked by it at first, scarcely able to believe it, thought he'd been mistaken. It appeared as if Judge Otis Brynn, for whom Boyd Garrison was campaigning so vigorously, and apparently at the risk of his life, was disappointed!

CHAPTER
TWO

Alone at the Alhambra Bar later that evening, Harlan nursed his drink and thought about Judge Brynn, wondering if he'd been mistaken. Brynn had pushed his way through the crowd later to shake his hand and thank him for his action. He'd been smiling and seemed sincere.

Boyd Garrison had eventually finished his speech, after the interruption, but Harlan hadn't listened to the rest of it. Disliking the publicity he'd received, he'd slipped away from the Bluebell Saloon, registered at a small hotel nearby, and had his supper there. The Alhambra adjoined the hotel restaurant, and he'd come in because he didn't want to spend the evening in a lonely hotel room.

Fred Barnhouse found him at the bar, and came up grumbling.

"Whole town's looking for you," the newspaper man scowled, "and here you're hiding out. Don't you know you're a hero, man?"

"Spent an hour searching every saloon in this town." Barnhouse scowled.

"You won't get any story out of me," Harlan told him, "but I'll buy you a drink."

"You won't buy me a drink, either," Barnhouse said. "Mr. Garrison's waiting for you at the hotel."

"Let him wait," Harlan said.

Fred Barnhouse looked at him curiously. "Garrison's the biggest man in this town, aside from William Andrews himself. He wants to thank you, man."

"Reckon he can find me here," Harlan said.

Barnhouse started to grin. "You're my kind of man," he said softly. "I'll bet you won't even take a reward if he offers you one."

"No," Harlan said.

"Not even if you were dead broke?"

"I'm close enough to that," Harlan confessed.

"How about a job?" Barnhouse wanted to know. "There's something else, mister."

Harlan twisted the liquor glass in his hand. "Reckon I still don't like this town," he said, "but I'd think about it."

"Then come along," the newspaper man urged him. "I think that's what Garrison has on his mind."

"Reckon I'll wait," Harlan said.

The tall, lean newspaper man had to have a drink after that. After he'd ordered he said:

"Every second deadbeat in this town is chasing after Boyd Garrison for a handout, or a job. You tell *him* to come down to see *you*."

"I didn't ask Garrison for a job," Harlan reminded him.

"I know," Barnhouse nodded, "and you don't want a reward for saving his life, and you wouldn't even cross the street to see him if he offered you a good job."

12

Harlan shrugged. He said thoughtfully:

"You running errands for Garrison, Barnhouse?"

Fred Barnhouse turned to look at him. Some of the color had left his lean face, the corners of his mouth were turned down, and all the humor had gone out of him.

"We don't have to talk about that," he said dully. "I'd met you on the street. Garrison asked me to look you up if I could find you. It was a favor."

Harlan nodded, but he was vaguely disappointed. It was as if Fred Barnhouse had shouted from the rooftops that he was Boyd Garrison's man. Garrison owned him, probably as he also owned Judge Otis Brynn of the silver hair and the unimpeachable reputation.

He wondered if Garrison owned Julia Brynn, too. He didn't think so. There had been a tilt to Miss Brynn's chin. She was not a woman you owned. She could be won, but not bought.

"I'll tell Garrison what you said," Barnhouse murmured when he'd finished his drink. "It's doubtful that he'll come to see you. When a man who's worth a half-million dollars wants to see somebody, he doesn't come across the road to see him. He just says the word."

"He didn't say it loud enough in this case," Harlan smiled. "I'll wait for him here, or he won't see me."

"Be good for this town if we had more men like you around," Barnhouse told him, and went out.

Harlan didn't think Garrison would come to see him, and he was surprised when ten minutes later, the copper magnate came through the bat-wing doors.

13

The saloon was fairly crowded at this time, and when Garrison came in they gave him a rousing welcome. Men pumped his hand and slapped his back as he pushed smiling through the crowd. There were avowals on all sides that they would support his candidates in the election on the morrow.

Harlan was sliding a bill across the bar to pay for his drink when Boyd Garrison said pleasantly at his elbow:

"I'll take care of that, Craig."

Harlan looked at him closely for the first time. They were the same height, and almost the same build, but here the resemblance stopped. Garrison's face, which probably once had been as lean and as hard as Harlan's, had become soft from easy living. The hand which rested on Harlan's was well-manicured, with no calluses, very white, in strange contrast to Harlan's hard, tanned hand.

"Reckon you can pay for this," Harlan told him, "if I pay for the next one."

"Sold." Garrison grinned. "I like your style, Craig." He ordered his drink from the bartender, then said, "I'm obliged to you for saving my life."

"Man had a gun on your back," Harlan said. "I saw it. That's all there was to it."

"Still," Garrison said thoughtfully, "I could have been a dead man tonight, lying on a wooden slab. It's something to think of. What can I do for you?"

"Not a thing," Harlan said. "You bought me a drink."

Garrison laughed. He had hazel eyes, classic features like a Greek god and curly golden-brown hair. Looking at him, Harlan could see how he was able to bind men to him — men like the ignorant miners who thronged around him in this saloon — but not men like Fred Barnhouse. Maybe the money had something to do with Barnhouse's allegiance.

"I don't buy a drink for a man who's saved my life," Garrison said, "and then say goodbye to him. I understand you were in the stage line business. Superintendent?"

"I owned the line," Harlan told him.

Garrison lifted his eyebrows slightly. "I should have known it," he said. "And you went broke."

"Railroad put us out of business," Harlan explained.

"Should have sold before they came near your territory. Didn't you know they were coming?"

"If I'd sold," Harlan explained, "the buyer would have had to stand the loss."

Boyd Garrison stared at him for a moment, and then smiled coolly. "You're in the wrong town with sentiments like those," he murmured. "You'd end up behind the rock pile."

"Figured on leaving tomorrow," Harlan told him.

"I can set you up here," Garrison said. "What is it you want?"

"Not a thing." Harlan said for the second time.

Garrison looked at him in the bar mirror, poured himself a drink from the bottle the bartender set before him, and then poured another for Harlan. He said easily:

"If you have five hundred dollars in your pockets, invest it in China Doll Mine stocks. In a month you can sell out for twenty-five hundred. That's a promise."

15

"You pushing China Doll Mine?" Harlan asked him.

"I happen to know they're going to strike a big vein of copper. Is that enough for you?"

"I don't want it," Harlan said.

"I'll loan you the five hundred," Garrison urged. "You pay me back when your stock shoots up. Fair enough?"

"I don't want it," Harlan said again. This was the way Boyd Garrison bought a man's soul. He was talking pennies now, but Harlan could visualize how it would be with a man who had a hundred thousand to invest, or twenty-five or fifty thousand, his life's earnings. Garrison could make a man rich, or he could make him poor. He had his finger on the pulse of this town. He had an interest in dozens of mines, in copper smelters, in timber to buttress his miles of underground workings, in politicians, judges, and newspapers.

Very possibly he had an interest in the China Doll Mine, and the rich vein of copper they'd struck was being concealed until Garrison was able to gobble up all the stock in sight on the China Doll — stock which would be worth ten times what he'd paid for it when the news of the strike reached the streets.

Garrison was saying laughingly, "You're either a sentimentalist, Craig, or a fool, and I don't believe you're a fool."

"I don't like that kind of money," Harlan told him.

"How about a job?" Garrison wanted to know. "You came here to get work, mister."

"Name it," Harlan said.

Boyd Garrison studied him thoughtfully. "You saw what nearly happened to me today," he stated. "I have enemies in this town as well as friends."

Harlan nodded.

"I need a bodyguard," Garrison said, "somebody to stand behind me with a gun. I'm not a coward, but I can't see in the back of my head. The job pays two hundred a month and keep. Will you take it?"

Harlan thought about it. The pay was very good, and it would give him a stake, which he needed badly. It was very evident, too, that Garrison needed someone to stand behind him.

"You are able to handle a gun?" Garrison asked.

"I carry a gun," Harlan nodded, "and I know how to use it."

"If you want the job," Garrison told him, "check in at the Empire Hotel tomorrow morning. You'll find a room reserved for you next to mine."

"What are my duties?" Harlan asked curiously.

"Keep me in sight." Garrison grinned. "See that I stay alive. It's a job; it has nothing to do with whether you like me or not." He added shrewdly, "You need a stake in this town, and there it is."

"I'll think about it," Harlan murmured.

"I might be tougher than you think," Garrison warned. "If anybody wants to put me out of the way, and they have to take care of you first, they'll do it. They'll squash you like a bug."

"They'll try," Harlan said.

"Think about it," Garrison urged. "I need an honest man around me."

He left, and Harlan remained at the bar, still considering Garrison's proposal. The pay was high, more than he could make elsewhere, and he would be earning the money. On the Coast there was no assurance that he could get anything.

The bartender passed by and said, "Great man, that Garrison. Man of the people. He's for the miner."

Harlan just nodded without comment. Having heard Garrison speak that afternoon, he could understand the man's popularity. Whether Garrison was for the miner or for Boyd Garrison was another matter.

Pushing away from the bar, Harlan went out to the street and stood on the edge of the walk, watching the crowds move by. There were at least thirty saloons and gambling houses along the main street alone, each one of them roaring. Rimrock was a boomtown at the base of the big hill, the richest hill on earth, and it seemed destined to eclipse all boomtowns before it.

Standing on the walk, Harlan heard a step on the wooden boards behind him, as someone came out of the saloon, and then a man said tersely:

"Backing the wrong horse, mister, if you back Garrison."

Harlan turned without haste. The man before him was solidly built, though not as tall as himself. He had a square-set face with heavy bones, and deep-set pale green eyes. His nose was flattened against his face, and his mouth was tough, uncompromising.

Harlan said easily, "I back who I please, friend."

"We'll ride you out of this town on a rail, too," the stranger told him.

"You might try." Harlan smiled.

"So you'll know me the next time," the heavy-set man said grimly, "I'm Griff Morgan. United Copper."

"William Andrews' boy," Harlan murmured. "I'll know you, mister."

He remembered that the United Copper Company was the rich outfit which was fighting Garrison, and the head of the company was William Andrews.

"If you're a cheap gun-hand he's bringing in to fight us," Morgan growled, "remember that anyone can fire a gun."

Harlan considered this statement. He hadn't been aware of the fact that Garrison was hiring gunmen for his war against United Copper. If it had come to that, the town of Rimrock was headed for real trouble.

"I'll remember it," Harlan smiled. "Anything else you want me to remember, Morgan?"

"You'll see, me around," Griff Morgan told him, and moved down the street.

Harlan watched him go, and then he stepped out onto the walk and moved in the opposite direction, pausing at the next corner when he reached the little shop which bore on the window:

"*Rimrock Miner*

Owner and Editor — Fred Barnhouse."

The lights were on in the shop. At the rear several men were setting type on a board. Barnhouse himself was at a desk at the front of the office.

Barnhouse looked up, and then snapped his pink arm-garters. Harlan could still see the resentment in the tall man's hazel eyes. Barnhouse hadn't liked Harlan's remarks in the saloon earlier in the evening.

"What's on your mind?" he asked.

Harlan sat down in the empty chair across the desk from the newspaper man.

"Garrison offered me a job as bodyguard for him," he said.

Barnhouse stared down at his desk. "You want me to print that?" he scowled. "Is that news?"

Harlan smiled. "Get off your high horse," he advised. "I made a nasty statement back in the Alhambra. I take it back."

Barnhouse was mollified immediately. Leaning back in the chair, he said, "It's advice you want, then."

Harlan shrugged. "Before I take any job," he said, "reckon I'd like to know what I'm running into."

The editor picked up a pencil and toyed with it, his long thin fingers turning the pencil around and around.

"Here's the set-up in a nutshell," he said quietly. "As you heard Garrison state this afternoon, United Copper owns this town, practically lock, stock and barrel. William Andrews is an Eastern financier who saw that copper was to be the big industrial metal. He came here with his millions and he bought up a lot of mines, smelters, everything else to go with it, including the souls of a great many men."

"Maybe I met one of them a few minutes ago," Harlan said thoughtfully. "Hard man — Griff Morgan."

"Andrews' front man in Rimrock," Barnhouse told him. "He's tough, and it's no bluff. Griff runs the Bengal Tiger Mine for Andrews. Biggest copper

20

producer on the hill. In Rimrock, United Copper is Griff Morgan. In New York, Boston, or Chicago, United Copper is William Andrews."

"And now Garrison," Harlan said.

"Garrison came in later. He's young, smart, and I think a lot tougher than most people imagine he is. Bought up a few mines, one of which is producing well, the High Dollar. He's United's only competitor worth mentioning in this town. He opposes United's candidates at the elections. He's providing the only competition United has in reducing copper ore. His smelter in Hell Valley is one of the big ones. He's been cutting his price per ton for refining copper ore, and he's been taking some business away from United which means that United has to chop him down."

"By means of a bullet from an empty saloon?" Harlan asked slowly. "They work that way in this town?"

Barnhouse shrugged. "Who can ever prove United was behind the attempted killing this afternoon? Garrison has other enemies besides William Andrews and Morgan."

Harlan thought of Judge Otis Brynn, and the expression on Brynn's face in the saloon.

"Garrison's been pretty rough in his dealings," Barnhouse was saying quietly. "Maybe not as rough and as ruthless as William Andrews, but there are men in this town who are financially ruined because they were in Garrison's way. Any one of them is liable to send a bullet through him."

"He'd need a bodyguard," Harlan said.

Barnhouse nodded. "I'm surprised he hasn't hired a man before."

"What happens tomorrow if Garrison gets his man elected?"

Barnhouse was staring at the desk top. "Judge Brynn?" he murmured. "After what you heard this afternoon, do you think there's any chance of his not being elected?"

"Not too much." Harlan smiled. "Your paper backing him?"

Barnhouse didn't look up from the desk. "If it comes to backing Garrison or William Andrews," he said, "I'd back Garrison."

Harlan knew how it was then. Barnhouse didn't have to support either man if he didn't want to, but the title on the plate glass window of this shop was a falsehood. Barnhouse did not own the *Rimrock Miner*. Garrison owned it, and Barnhouse printed what Garrison wanted him to print.

"When Otis Brynn is elected," Fred Barnhouse was saying slowly, "I'm expecting fireworks of one sort or another."

Harlan could well imagine that Boyd Garrison, with public opinion, the local newspaper, and the judge of the district court behind, would ride the lead horse.

"Is Garrison hiring gunmen to back his play?" Harlan asked next.

Barnhouse stared at him. "I wasn't aware of that," he said.

"Morgan seemed to think he was."

"I haven't heard," Barnhouse said. "You hiring on as bodyguard for him?"

Harlan didn't know, and then his mind was made up for him very abruptly.

A tiny bell tinkled behind him as the door was opened, and when he turned his head to see who was coming in, he looked at the most beautiful woman he'd ever seen in his life. He took one look at her, and he knew that he was remaining in Rimrock, and that he was taking the job Boyd Garrison had offered him.

CHAPTER
THREE

The woman was tall, taller than Julia Brynn, and she had copper-colored hair. Her eyes were turquoise, large, well-spaced, and her nose was small and perfectly formed. She wore a green velvet dress which brought out the color of her hair, and her hat, too, was of green velvet with a darker green feather in it, a rather saucy little hat.

Both men stood up as she came in, and Harlan took off his hat, backing away a little from Barnhouse's desk.

"I didn't mean to intrude," the girl said, and the voice was low, musical, fitting her exactly. "Are you open for business at this hour?"

"What can I do for you?" Barnhouse asked. "I am the editor of the *Rimrock Miner*."

The girl glanced curiously at Harlan, giving him the faintest of smiles, and then she stated her business. She desired to put a small advertisement in the *Miner*, and she told Barnhouse what it was as Harlan moved over to a pile of last week's papers and glanced through one of them. He could not help overhearing her.

Her name was Marcia Reynolds, and she wanted to put an advertisement in the *Miner* that she was opening a small dress shop in Rimrock. She was recently from Chicago, and she'd brought with her some of the latest models for the fashionable ladies of Rimrock.

Harlan presumed there were some fashionable ladies in Rimrock, wives of mine superintendents and engineers, mine owners' wives who preferred to live with their husbands in Rimrock rather than alone in more civilized towns.

"You are new in Rimrock?" Fred Barnhouse asked her.

"I arrived from Chicago yesterday," Miss Reynolds informed him.

"And how do you like our town?"

"It could be cleaner," Marcia Reynolds chuckled, "but I knew I was coming to a mining town. I'll have to take the soot with the profits."

"A good philosophy," Barnhouse agreed. "You are staying at the Grant House?"

"The Grant House." It was the same hotel at which Harlan had registered for a room, one of the smaller, less pretentious hotels in booming Rimrock.

"Copies of the *Miner* and your bill will be mailed to the Grant House, Miss Reynolds," Barnhouse told her. "We wish you success in your enterprise."

"Thank you." The tall girl smiled. As she turned toward the door, Harlan stepped in that direction to open it for her.

He said, "I'm staying at the Grant House, Miss Reynolds. Might be safer if someone walked back with you. Plenty of drunks on the street at night."

Fred Barnhouse said from the desk, "Harlan Craig, Miss Reynolds. Stage line man from the Coast."

"I would appreciate an escort, Mr. Craig," Marcia Reynolds murmured. "You are very kind."

Harlan put on his hat as she passed through the door, nodding back to Fred Barnhouse. Barnhouse said softly to Harlan:

"You accepting Garrison's job, Craig?"

"I wouldn't be surprised," Harlan told him, and a slow grin spread across Barnhouse's lean face.

Out on the street, Marcia Reynolds said curiously, "You are acquainted with Mr. Garrison, Mr. Craig?"

"Met him," Harlan told her. "He offered me a job — as bodyguard."

"How interesting," she said. "You are big enough, Mr. Craig."

He walked beside her down the street.

"I have heard a great deal of talk concerning Mr. Garrison," the girl said. "He's a big figure even in Chicago."

"Made his mark." Harlan nodded. "Chicago your town?"

"Chicago, New York, Philadelphia," she said. "I've been around."

"Dress shops?" he asked.

"More or less. I've been on my own since Mother died three years ago."

He figured her age to be about twenty-three or four, and she did not have a ring on her finger, which was surprising. A girl like this could have had her pick even in Chicago or New York.

"I heard Mr. Garrison's speech this afternoon," Miss Reynolds said. "I think it's wonderful the way he is fighting the big copper trust."

Harlan wondered what kind of trust Garrison would set up if United Copper were bested and driven out of Rimrock. His mines paid the best wages in town, and his smelter was a godsend to the independent mine owners who had been hung up by United Copper, but Boyd Garrison was fighting a rival company. If there were no opposition, Harlan wondered if Garrison would be so charitable.

"You won't be living at the Grant House when you work for Mr. Garrison?" Miss Reynolds asked as they were entering their hotel.

"Garrison's at the Empire," Harlan explained. "He's reserved a room for me there."

"Your work will be dangerous."

Harlan shrugged. "It could be," he agreed.

"Why do you do it?"

"Why do you sell dresses?" he countered.

In the lobby of the Grant House Harlan saw the town marshal, Cole McAfee, coiled up in a chair near the desk. McAfee had a cigar going, and he was evidently waiting for someone. Harlan had the suspicion that it was himself. McAfee lifted a finger to him, and he remained in the chair as Harlan paused at the foot of the stairs which led to the second floor. His own room was down a corridor on the first floor of the building.

Marcia Reynolds smiled. "I'm obliged to you for walking me home."

"My pleasure," Harlan told her. "I'll see you around."

"Of course," she said, and went up the stairs.

McAfee got up from his chair as Harlan turned around, and stood there waiting for Harlan to come back.

"Something on your mind, Marshal?" Harlan asked him.

"Just the man who tried to kill Boyd Garrison." McAfee sighed. "Reckon everybody else can forget about it. The law has to search for the attempted killer."

"Get nothing out of me." Harlan smiled. "I've been in this town ten hours. I know Barnhouse, the newspaper man, and I met Garrison and Griff Morgan after the shooting."

"You meet nice people," McAfee said, looking toward the stairs.

"Met her in Barnhouse's office," Harlan explained. "Figured somebody should escort her back to the hotel at night."

McAfee took the cigar from his mouth and looked at it. "You didn't get too good a look at this hombre tried to shoot Garrison?"

Harlan shook his head. "I fell as I went through the door. It was only a half-dozen steps to the rear door. He went out quick."

"You wouldn't recognize him again?"

"Never saw his face," Harlan said.

McAfee puffed on the cigar. "It strike you that the chap who tried to kill Garrison might not feel so friendly to you now?"

Harlan smiled. "I'll sleep tonight," he said.

"And I'd be careful," McAfee warned. "You're in a tough town, mister."

"I've been in tough towns before," Harlan told him.

"Never in a town where the stakes were so high," McAfee said thoughtfully. "These boys aren't playing penny ante, Craig. This is for millions. You don't even stack up in this deal."

"Then they won't bother me." Harlan smiled.

"You've already gotten in somebody's way," the town marshal informed him. "When you play a card, mister, you can't take it back."

"Who am I supposed to watch?" Harlan grinned.

"In this town, anybody," McAfee stated. "When they're able to pay out fifty or a hundred thousand dollars to put someone out of the way, I wouldn't trust my own brother."

"So I couldn't trust you, either."

"If I were in your boots," McAfee said soberly, "I wouldn't trust me, either."

"It's a hard life," Harlan smiled. "Keep me alive as long as you can, Marshal."

McAfee left the lobby, and Harlan turned down the corridor which led to his room at the far end. The night was still young, but he was tired, and it had been a long day, and he hadn't slept on the train the night before.

Off in the distance, through the walls of the hotel, he could hear the dull pounding of stamp mills reducing silver ore. The sulphur smell from the copper smelters was inside the hotel, also, but he noticed that he'd become more or less accustomed to it during the day, and it was not so bad now.

His room was the last one at the end of a corridor which was dimly lighted by two oil lamps in brackets on the walls. It had been one of the few remaining rooms in the hotel.

Reaching the door, Harlan felt for the key in his pocket. He was still thinking of Cole McAfee's warning when he turned the key in the keyhole and opened the door of the darkened room.

He remembered that the lamp was on a table to the left of the door, and all he had to do was feel for it, strike a match, and touch it to the wick.

He never touched the lamp, however, because there was something the matter with this room. For one moment he was unable to account for the change, and then he smelled it again — fresh tobacco smoke.

He remembered that he hadn't smoked when he'd first entered the room earlier in the evening, and he'd only stayed a few minutes before going out to eat. The room then had been free of tobacco smoke.

Reacting immediately, Harlan closed the door with a sweep of his hand and sank down to the floor, at the same time feeling for the gun inside his coat. Someone had either been in this room very recently, or was still here, probably with a gun, waiting for him to strike that match and light the lamp.

Sitting on the floor in complete darkness, he listened carefully, trying to remember the exact dimensions of this little hotel room, and every object of furniture in it. He fancied that he could hear another man breathing, but he was not sure. In the darkness the imagination could play tricks.

The bed was straight ahead of him, probably five feet away. To the right of the bed was a dresser with the usual wash basin and pitcher of water. There was a chair on the left side of the bed, and another chair against the wall on the other side of the little table which held the lamp.

That was all. There was no closet for clothes, no alcove in which a man could hide. To the left of the bed was the lone window in the room. He hadn't looked out the window because at the time he'd rented the room it had already been dark, but he assumed from the location of the room that this window opened on the rear of the hotel, undoubtedly a vacant, refuse-strewn lot.

A man could very easily pry open a window on the ground floor if he wanted entry, or a man with any amount of skill could gain access with the use of a hairpin or a skeleton key. The lock on the door was flimsy.

Sliding back the hammer of the Smith & Wesson noiselessly, Harlan waited, knowing that he'd confused his man if he were still in the room. The first man to shoot blindly now would reveal his position by the flash of the gun.

Very carefully, Harlan lowered his body toward the floor, turning so that he came to rest on his stomach and elbows, the gun in his right hand pointing at a spot below the window.

Five minutes had gone by since he'd dropped to the floor after smelling the smoke. Another five went by as he lay on the floor. He was almost positive now that he could hear another man breathing in the room. Several times he held his own breath, listening intently. The killer was still there, patiently waiting for him to concede that he'd made a mistake and strike the match which would be his death warrant.

Harlan resolved to remain where he was if he had to live here till morning. He grinned, thinking of the ludicrousness of the situation. It would be at least nine hours till the first gray light of dawn came in around the drawn shade. The man who broke first would probably die.

CHAPTER
FOUR

Thirty minutes passed before Harlan heard the first definite movement in the room, proving to him that he was not alone. The sound of a man's breathing could have been his imagination, but this was not. Someone had shifted his weight to ease an aching bone or muscle.

The sound had come from the left side of the bed near the window. He started to feel about cautiously with his left hand after drawing himself up on hands and knees. Eventually, moving his hand very slowly, he came in contact with the leg of the table by the door, and he knew what he could do.

Bracing himself, he took a deep breath, and then up-ended the table. The lamp slid to the floor with a crash, and immediately the gun started to bark from the opposite side of the room. There were three quick shots, and then Harlan fired at the flash of the gun.

A woman started to scream in a room nearby, and then the killer who'd been firing his lead into the wall where he'd thought Harlan was standing went through the opened window, taking the shade with him.

Harlan leaped to his feet and lunged forward. He wasn't prepared for the fact that the bed had been moved a few feet by the killer, who'd been half-concealed behind it.

His right hip hit the corner of the bed and he stumbled, nearly falling to the floor. By the time he righted himself, the other man was through the window.

Anger driving through him, Harlan tore through the opening himself, and as his boots touched the ground outside, he could hear his man moving across the back yard toward a low shed-like building in the rear.

The light here was poor, but better than it had been in the bedroom, and Harlan could see him vaguely as he ran. He fired one quick shot and then took after him, not knowing whether he'd nicked his man or not.

He could hear windows opening in the rear of the hotel, and a man was shouting:

"It's a gunfight!"

He ran hard, stumbling through the litter in the yard, coming to a low wooden fence which had a break in it. The killer had gone through the break in the fence and rounded the corner of the shed on the other side. He'd probably come in here the same way, and knew his way around.

Harlan went through the fence, ripping another board loose with his shoulder as he went by. A horse and rider tore out of the shed as Harlan came up to it, and the killer fired at him at a distance of less than a dozen feet.

The moving horse made his gun unsteady, and the slug went through Harlan's coat. Steadying his gun carefully, Harlan fired once, and the killer tumbled from the saddle, his body hitting the dirt with a sickening thud. The horse ran on another thirty yards, and then slowed down to a walk.

Gun in hand, Harlan moved forward toward the fallen man, not sure if he were dead or playing possum. When he was ten feet away he saw metal gleaming in the dust, and he picked up a six-gun, knowing then that his shot had taken effect. The killer was now unarmed, and either dead or badly wounded.

Men were coming up an alley from the main street. There were others who'd come out into the back yard of the hotel. He heard Cole McAfee's sharp voice:

"What's happening here?"

Straightening up with the gun in his hand, Harlan said briefly, "This way, McAfee."

Cole McAfee came through the break in the fence and moved down toward him slowly.

"Who's this?" he asked.

Harlan struck a match and held it up to his face, and heard the marshal's low grunt as he bent down to roll over the body of the man he'd hit.

"Figured you were down for the night." McAfee scowled. "What do you have here?"

"Tried to do me in," Harlan explained. "Hiding in my room with a six-gun on me. I chased him out here and dropped him from his horse."

McAfee knelt down as Harlan rolled the body over and held the match to the face. The man on the ground had a narrow hatchet face, with a pointed chin and a wide, thin mouth. A bullet, probably the one Harlan had fired at him in the hotel room, had grazed his right cheekbone, leaving a livid bruise and a little blood, but the bullet which had killed him had gone through his body. The front of his gray flannel shirt was staining red. He was dead, his features already settling in death.

The match went out, and Harlan straightened up.

"You shoot straight," McAfee said.

"Know him?" Harlan asked.

The town marshal looked down at the dead man. "Goes by the name of Sam Feeney, which means nothing to you."

"No," Harlan said. "Who sent him?"

"Man who sent somebody after Boyd Garrison. Maybe the same hombre was sent out both times. Recognize him?"

"Can't say," Harlan said grimly. He had no sympathy for the dead killer, lying in the dust. This man had waited for him patiently, soberly, to kill him, a total stranger. He'd done it for money.

"Feeney was a drifter in this town," McAfee was saying. "Hundred like him around. Pay him the right amount, and he'd slit his own brother's throat."

"Griff Morgan know him?" Harlan asked.

McAfee laughed shortly. "You can't figure it that way, mister," he said. "Griff knows a lot of people. You'll never prove he, or United Copper, paid this dog to shoot you down."

They started down the alley toward the street, and McAfee dispatched a man to bring up the coroner.

Harlan said, "It wasn't you, anyway, was it?"

"Wasn't me," McAfee agreed, "not this time."

Fred Barnhouse, coming up from his office to cover the shooting, met them as they came out of the alley.

"Killing?" he said to McAfee, and he looked at Harlan curiously.

"This one did it," the marshal told him, nodding toward Harlan. "Sam Feeney tried to shoot him up in his room. Sam picked the wrong man."

"You're still making news in this town," Barnhouse observed, and then he said to McAfee, "You know Craig here is signing up as Boyd Garrison's bodyguard?"

"Reckon that's more news," McAfee murmured. "How long you expect to live, Craig?"

"Might depend upon Griff Morgan," Harlan said. "Where can I find him?"

"Now?" Barnhouse asked.

"Now," Harlan nodded.

"He'd be in the Casino," McAfee observed. "All the big mine operators spend their time in the Casino. Biggest gambling house in town. You figure on shooting Morgan up?"

"Not tonight," Harlan smiled. "It'll be talk tonight."

"Reckon I'd like to hear this," McAfee murmured. "Griff Morgan don't take talk from the devil himself."

"We'll see," Harlan said, and they walked in the direction of the Casino two blocks down along the main street.

"William Andrews came to town tonight on the late westbound," Barnhouse was saying. "You'll find him there, too, Craig. You aim to tell him off?"

Harlan shrugged. "Morgan first," he said.

The Casino was on the second floor, and they had access to it through a door adjoining one of the saloons. They went up the narrow flight of stairs, and an attendant greeted them cordially as they entered.

The man grinned at McAfee. "Bucking the tiger, Marshal?"

"Not me." McAfee smiled. "Him." He pointed to Harlan.

It was the most elaborate set-up Harlan had ever seen. The Casino occupied the entire floor of the building. The mahogany bar against the rear wall was not too large, but ornate. Three bartenders operated behind the bar.

There were no miners here. These men were well-dressed, quiet-spoken. They sat at the card tables or they stood around the roulette wheel, their faces expressionless.

"Man lost ten thousand last week," Barnhouse said, "on a single turn of a card. Boyd Garrison won the major share of the High Dollar Mine in here."

Harlan spotted Garrison sitting at one of the card tables across the room. The unimpeachable Judge Otis Brynn was at the same table, and there was a shine to Brynn's smooth face. He'd been drinking, probably more than he should.

Looking at him, and looking at Garrison, Harlan knew how it was with them. Garrison had picked Judge Brynn from the ash heap, and was setting him up as a judge in the district. It was Garrison's money, and Garrison's newspaper, and the Garrison personality, which would sweep Judge Brynn into office on the morrow. Everlastingly, Otis Brynn would have to remember that.

Harlan wondered how much Julia Brynn knew about this, or suspected. He wondered if her supposed engagement to Boyd Garrison were based upon this debt her father owed to the man who was setting him on his feet again.

Fred Barnhouse was saying, "Morgan's at the keno table, Craig, but I think you're a fool to make an issue out of this. It won't get you anywhere."

"I'll let him know I'm still alive," Harlan murmured, "if it means anything to him."

He saw Garrison look up, and then lift a friendly hand to him as he started to move toward the keno table where Griff Morgan was standing with a half-dozen other men. Judge Brynn looked up also, and he watched Harlan thoughtfully.

Fred Barnhouse drifted away as Harlan started toward Morgan, and Cole McAfee went with him. McAfee said softly as they walked:

"There'll be no gunplay here, mister. You know that."

"This is talk," Harlan said.

"Talk is cheap," McAfee smiled, "and it never hurt anybody."

Garrison pushed back his chair a little as he saw Harlan moving in Griff Morgan's direction. Morgan saw him coming, too, and his hard, wide face tightened.

Harlan said to him as he came up, "Like to see you at the bar, Morgan."

"What about?" Morgan snapped.

Cole McAfee answered the question. "About poor Sam Feeney who was shot up by Craig ten minutes ago."

"What have I got to do with Sam Feeney?" Morgan rasped.

"Somebody sent Feeney to shoot me up," Harlan stated. "Feeney waited in my hotel room with a gun. I don't know Feeney, and Feeney doesn't know me, which means that somebody paid Feeney to wait there."

"I paid him," Griff Morgan sneered. "Is that it?"

"I'm asking," Harlan said.

He had to admit that Morgan was either putting on a great act, or he was completely innocent.

"I'll make it very plain for you," Morgan snarled. "When I want you dead, Craig, I'll come after you myself. I won't send a cutthroat. You have my word for that."

"You have my word for this." Harlan smiled. "I'll be waiting for you."

Boyd Garrison had gotten up from the card table and was moving toward them as they spoke. He said casually as he came up, "Trouble here, gentlemen?"

"Just talkin'," McAfee told him. "One way and another."

"You have any more to say, Craig?" Morgan snapped.

"That's it," Harlan told him. "Wanted you to know I was still alive, and aim to be for a long time."

"You won't," Griff Morgan growled, "with that kind of talk."

He turned back to his game, and Harlan moved away toward the bar with Cole McAfee and Garrison. Garrison said as they walked:

"Have you been considering my offer, Craig?"

"Accepted it," Harlan told him.

"Reckon he's already in business." McAfee smiled. "Sam Feeney was paid to kill him tonight in his hotel room. Craig here figures Morgan might know something about it."

"Who is Sam Feeney?" Garrison wanted to know.

"A ten-dollar killer," McAfee explained. "He ain't important. Besides, Craig here shot him clear to Boot Hill."

Garrison lifted his eyebrows as they paused at the bar. "Evidently I picked the right man,'" he said. "Glad to have you with us, Craig. Your salary will start as of tonight."

Harlan shrugged.

"Your job, of course," Garrison went on smoothly, "is to keep me alive." He added softly, "And also yourself."

CHAPTER
FIVE

Judge Otis Brynn won his election by a landslide the next day, and early that evening Harlan Craig met Julia Brynn for the first time, at a victory celebration in the Empire Hotel dining room.

Boyd Garrison seemed highly elated over the victory. There was flush on his face, and his voice was unnaturally loud. He hadn't been drinking, and Harlan knew that he never drank to the point of intoxication.

Garrison had said to Miss Brynn, "Julia, meet Harlan Craig. He's working with us."

He moved off then, leaving them alone. The room was crowded with people, and Garrison had to greet them all.

Julia Brynn was wearing a maroon dress with a low neck, and her rich brown hair was done up in a bunch at the back. She looked at Harlan quizzically, and said, "You are new in this town, Mr. Craig."

"Arrived yesterday," Harlan told her.

"In the mining business?"

"I'm Mr. Garrison's bodyguard," Harlan stated, and he saw her eyes widen a little.

"It's as bad as that?" she murmured.

"You saw what happened yesterday," he told her.

"I know," she said. "It is regrettable that there are such men in Rimrock."

He could see from the way she spoke that she didn't know. She was not in on Boyd Garrison's deals. She did not know that her father, by accepting Garrison's help, no longer had a soul he could call his own. In her mind Garrison was gallantly coming to the aid of her father with the purest of motives.

Harlan glanced in the direction of one of the tables where Judge Brynn sat with several other men, a wine glass in his hand, a thoughtful expression on his face. Otis Brynn was already somewhat under the weather, and the night was young. His mouth was looser than it should have been, and his eyes slightly glazed. While he could undoubtedly walk a chalk line if he had to, Harlan was convinced he'd imbibed too freely tonight in celebrating his victory.

"You must be proud of your father," Harlan said, "but I wouldn't say that this was his first political victory."

"He was a judge in Indiana before we came out here," Julia Brynn told him, and he saw her glance rather worriedly in her father's direction.

It was apparent that she knew about the drinking, and had been concerned about it before. Harlan wondered whether this had been the cause of Brynn's downfall, and hence his dependency upon Boyd Garrison.

"We owe a great deal to Mr. Garrison for Father's election," Miss Brynn was saying.

"Every man needs friends." Harlan smiled faintly.

He watched Garrison moving around the room, talking with groups of men, smiling, shaking hands, giving each man his personal attention. Garrison evidently knew the value of friends, also, and how to use them.

Fred Barnhouse was in the room, sitting at one of the tables alone, and when Miss Brynn excused herself and turned to speak to someone else, Harlan dropped into a chair next to the newspaper man.

"A great victory." Barnhouse scowled. "A great and glorious victory over United Copper and William Andrews."

"What would Andrews have done if he'd gotten his candidates into office?" Harlan asked curiously.

"Maybe no worse than Garrison," Barnhouse smiled grimly, "but we shall see." He changed the subject deftly. "Have you seen your friend, Miss Reynolds?"

"Not since I met her in your office," Harlan told him.

"Rather an attractive girl," Barnhouse observed.

"I think so," Harlan agreed.

"And what do you think of Miss Brynn?"

Harlan didn't look at the tall man directly, but he knew that Barnhouse was watching him closely. He understood the reason for the question, also. Barnhouse was in love with Julia Brynn, and this was the reason he remained in Rimrock, taking Garrison's orders when he could have gone somewhere else after Garrison had bought him out.

"I would say," Harlan smiled, "that Miss Brynn is equally attractive."

44

Barnhouse didn't say anything to that. He sat at the table, drumming with his fingers on the tablecloth, a slight frown on his face, watching Boyd Garrison.

Harlan said to him, "You think the fireworks will start now that Garrison has his own judge on the bench?"

"I am anticipating it." Barnhouse nodded. "He's had a staff of surveyors working on the hill the past few weeks. He's up to something, but I don't know what it is."

"There are no loose claims upon the hill?" Harlan asked.

Barnhouse laughed dryly. "Every foot of the big hill was staked out ten years ago."

He stood up suddenly, and said, "Here's trouble."

Harlan turned to look, and saw a big, red-haired man, who'd evidently just come in from the street, talking with Boyd Garrison. They were in a corner off by themselves, and the red-haired man was gesticulating as he spoke.

"That's Ed Nicholson, mine superintendent at Garrison's High Dollar Mine," Barnhouse said softly, "and I'd say they ran up against something."

Garrison was looking in Harlan's direction now, and Fred Barnhouse said, "Where there's trouble, Craig, that's where you fit in."

Harlan moved across the room, walking around groups of men and around tables, Barnhouse following him.

When they reached Garrison, the mine operator turned and said briefly, "We've run into a little trouble at the High Dollar Mine. I'm going down there now. I don't know whether this covers your job, Craig."

"Reckon I'll go," Harlan said.

Garrison had a word with Judge Brynn and with Julia, and then came back to where they were waiting at the door. Harlan had already shaken hands with Ed Nicholson, and the big red-head had eyed him thoughtfully, neither friendliness nor animosity in his eyes.

Barnhouse, who evidently was going along for the news, said, "What's the trouble, Ed?"

"Bengal Tiger miners broke into a stope in the High Dollar," the superintendent explained. "There's been some fighting. Griff Morgan is down there with them."

The four men left the building, Garrison and Nicholson up ahead, Harlan coming behind with Fred Barnhouse.

"Bengal Tiger Mine is United Copper property," Barnhouse explained as they hurried up the street. "It adjoins Garrison's High Dollar. Every once in a while one crew breaks into a stope being worked by a crew from a rival mine. Both accuse the other of trespassing, and it takes surveyors, lawyers, and law courts to settle the matter." He added dryly, "I'd say, however, that most matters are settled out of court with miners using pick handles on each other's heads, and with steam hoses, and not infrequently with guns."

"It's a rough town," Harlan observed.

"You haven't seen it yet," the newspaper man growled, "until you get underground."

46

There was a stable halfway down the street where Nicholson had left his horse. Boyd Garrison procured three more horses, and in a few minutes they were riding north out of town, headed for the copper mines.

It was a half-mile out of Rimrock to the shaft of the High Dollar Mine. A surface worker took their horses as they dismounted and hurried to the cage which would lower them into the earth.

Two miners with carbide lamps on their hats stepped into the cage with him. Nicholson had picked up several lanterns and a rifle. He handed one of the lanterns to Harlan, who took it without a word. The rifle Nicholson carried was a late model Winchester.

As they stepped into the cage the big red-head said to Harlan, "You armed, Craig?"

"I have a gun," Harlan acknowledged. He touched the side of his coat.

"He knows how to use it, too," Barnhouse added.

Nicholson didn't say anything to that.

A bell rang, and the cage started to sink down into the shaft. It was Harlan's first experience going underground, and he caught his breath for the moment as the cage dropped steadily downward, the rough dirt and rock walls sliding by in the murky light of the lanterns and the miners' lamps.

"What level?" Garrison asked.

"Tenth," Nicholson told him.

Harlan glanced at Barnhouse, and the newspaper man said succinctly, "We're going down twelve hundred feet or so."

At the tenth level the cage stopped and they stepped out into a tunnel ribbed with heavy timbers. Under an overhang a short distance away Harlan could see the stalls for the mules which pulled the ore cars. There were several animals in the stalls, and a boy was watering them.

In the distance they could hear what sounded like the dull, hollow boom of guns underground,

"Were they shooting before?" Garrison asked as they hurried down along the narrow ore car tracks.

"Just words before," Nicholson told him. "Reckon they're gettin' rough, Mr. Garrison."

They proceeded about five hundred feet down along the tunnel, the sound of gunfire coming closer as they proceeded, and then, rounding a bend in the tunnel, they came upon a low rock barricade which had been set up across the tunnel floor.

A half-dozen miners crouched behind the barricade, and two of them had rifles. A rifle bullet ricocheted off the wall and went whining down the tunnel, and Boyd Garrison yelled:

"Everybody down!"

They dropped behind the barricade, and Harlan slipped the Smith & Wesson from the holster.

"They play rough down here," Barnhouse said sourly. "I'm just here for the news."

"Who opened fire first?" Garrison asked of one of the miners.

"They did, Mr. Garrison," the miner told him. "We piled up these rocks like Nicholson told us, an' then

Griff Morgan warned us to get out. When we didn't, one of 'em sent a bullet down here."

"Hold your fire," Garrison told him, and then he called down the murky tunnel, "Morgan? You there?"

"You're darn right," Morgan's voice came back, hard and rasping. "Your crew is fifty feet into the Bengal Tiger, Garrison. Move your crew out and seal up this tunnel."

"We'll move," Garrison retorted, "when the court decides that we're to move, and not before."

Crouching beside him, Harlan Craig realized now how important it was for Garrison to have a man on the bench in the district court who owed him something, even his office.

"You've already taken fifty thousand dollars worth of ore out of this tunnel," Griff Morgan snapped, "and you'll take another fifty thousand while your crooked judge is making a decision. You'll move your men out now, or you'll move them out, dead, in the morning."

"Tell him to try and move us," Nicholson retorted. "He'll wish he hadn't."

"Is there an air pipe back there?" Garrison asked him.

"Reckon there is," the superintendent chuckled.

"You know what to do," Garrison said.

Nicholson crawled back around the bend of the tunnel without another word.

Griff Morgan called from the darkness beyond, "What are you going to do, Garrison? We have another dozen toughs from town arriving here any minute. We're coming after you."

Garrison said blandly, "Give us ten minutes to think it over, Morgan."

Harlan watched him turn and lean his back against the rocks, and then grin at Fred Barnhouse.

"What's going to happen?" Harlan asked curiously.

"Slack lime down the air pipe," Barnhouse told him. "It's an old and pleasant custom. Evidently Griff doesn't know we have an airpipe down there. When that powdered lime starts circulating at the other end of the tunnel, he'll have to get back into his own mine. There's no living with it."

"It's not dangerous," Garrison observed. "We just want to drive them out."

"What then?" Harlan asked.

"We block up that hole through which they came," Garrison told him, "and we leave a dozen men in this tunnel with rifles."

"And you go on mining copper ore," Barnhouse added softly.

"Why not?" Garrison asked, and there was some sharpness in his voice as he glanced over at the tall newspaper man whose thin face looked haggard in the dim, flickering light of lamps and lanterns.

"Why not, indeed?" Barnhouse shrugged. "If William Andrews and Griff Morgan, had you over the same barrel they wouldn't let you up."

"Are we mining Bengal Tiger ore?" Harlan asked.

"Who knows?" Garrison grinned. "Copper ore in the big hill is for the man who can dig it. We're underground and we're following a copper vein. If that vein extends into the claim owned by a neighboring mine owner, we have the legal right to follow the vein and take out ore until it peters out."

"Only one little difficulty," Barnhouse added dryly. "There are a great many faults underground. A vein is broken and starts again somewhere else, or maybe it's a new vein which another mine owner is working. You can see the necessity, Craig, for a staff of lawyers and mining experts. A big mine operator couldn't get along without them."

"Nor," Harlan said thoughtfully, "a judge on the bench who happens to be a friend."

"Friends are always helpful," Garrison chuckled. "Is it not so, Harlan?"

Harlan didn't say anything to that. He didn't like to think of Julia Brynn mixed up in a thing like this. She was too fine and decent a girl.

Five minutes after Nicholson left them they could hear men begin to cough at the other end of the tunnel.

Someone cursed and yelled, "Slack lime!"

"Keep the rifles ready," Garrison ordered, "in case they charge us."

Griff Morgan roared down the tunnel, "We'll be back, Garrison. You can gamble on that."

There was more coughing and cursing, and they could hear men moving over loose rock. The light from their own carbide lamps and lanterns extended only a short distance down the tunnel. Morgan's Bengal Tiger crew were just around a bend in the tunnel. They could see the light from their lamps, but the men were concealed around the bend. The intervening space lay in darkness.

"They're getting out," Barnhouse said. "You won this time, Garrison."

They had to retreat themselves, because the slack lime powder was drifting in their direction, filling the tunnel. Harlan could feel it burning his throat and nostrils.

Nicholson stepped out of the cage, when they reached it, with half a dozen men equipped with crude masks, and all of them carrying rifles.

"We'll work on that hole before they can come near it," Nicholson said to Garrison. "I think we'll be able to start drilling again in the morning."

"Put double crews down here from now on," Garrison ordered. "Three shifts a day, and drive them."

"William Andrews will have a court order on you in the morning to stop operations in the High Dollar," Barnhouse observed.

"I'll worry about the court order," Garrison told him.

They went up in the cage, and when Harlan stepped out again on solid ground with the stars overhead, he took a deep breath.

"Don't like it down there?" Barnhouse said as he touched a match to a cigar.

"I'll stay up here," Harlan told him.

"I'll stay with you." Barnhouse smiled.

They rode back to Rimrock, Boyd Garrison moving slightly ahead of Harlan and the newspaper man, his head bent a little as if in thought.

Harlan nodded toward him, and said softly to Barnhouse, "You think it's leading up to a big fight?"

"Been coming for a long time," Barnhouse replied. "Now with Judge Brynn on the bench it's come to a head. Brynn will back Garrison on this and a lot of other disputes. Mr. Andrews' only alternate is to fight — with brickbats, slack lime, hot steam, and guns."

"Underground," Harlan scowled. "A heck of a way to fight."

"You moving out, then?" Barnhouse asked curiously.

Harlan thought of Marcia Reynolds, who'd just come to Rimrock, and then of Julia Brynn with the dark brown hair and eyes, and the quiet, gentle manner.

"Reckon I'll stay awhile," he said. "I'm a curious man."

"Curious men can sometimes be dead men," Barnhouse told him. "You almost found that out last night, mister."

Harlan glanced down at the lights of Rimrock as they descended the big hill, moving down one of the many trails.

"Every man dies," he said.

CHAPTER
SIX

In town as they were dismounting outside the livery stable, Boyd Garrison said to Harlan, "I have a conference with some of my surveyors up in my quarters, Craig. You won't have to come along."

Harlan nodded. "Be careful," he warned. "This town's getting rough."

Garrison smiled faintly. "You wouldn't like to see me killed?" he asked.

"I wouldn't like to lose my job, either," Harlan told him, and Garrison's smile turned into a grin.

"We understand each other," he said softly.

"You're a pair," Fred Barnhouse murmured as he walked down the livery stable alley with Harlan, and Garrison went in through the back entrance of the Empire House.

"Reckon we'll get along," Harlan said. "You heading back to your office to write this up?"

"I'll get it down on paper," Barnhouse replied, "while its fresh."

At the head of the alley they parted, and Harlan turned in the direction of the Empire Hotel porch. He saw Sheriff McAfee sitting on the top step, his hat pushed back on his head, a half-smoked cigar in his mouth.

"People ridin' all over town." McAfee scowled. "Nobody thinks to notify the marshal. What the devil's goin' on around here, Craig?"

"Reckon you missed the boat." Harlan grinned. "Little excitement up in the High Dollar Mine."

"Gun play?" McAfee asked curiously.

"They use slack lime around here," Harlan told him. "No one was killed or even hurt as far as I know. You the law underground, too?"

"Underground, on the ground, or above the ground," McAfee said thinly. "I'd like this town to remember that."

"Tell that to Boyd Garrison and Griff Morgan." Harlan smiled. "You know where I get my orders."

"One of 'em stealing ore from the other?" Cole McAfee wanted to know.

"That's how it sounded down there," Harlan agreed.

"Tomorrow," McAfee growled, "I have a court order to close the High Dollar, or the Bengal Tiger, one or the other. In twenty-four hours the order is rescinded, and they go on like before, only the fighting is in court with staffs of lawyers."

"Better than with guns," Harlan told him.

"The guns will come," McAfee said gloomily, "when the lawyers run out of words. That's what worries me. With the kind of money they throw around in this town, they can bring in armies of the best gunslingers in the West." He looked at Harlan thoughtfully, and added, "Like you, for instance."

"I'm not a gunslinger," Harlan said. "I'm protection for Boyd Garrison."

"And where do you draw the line," McAfee asked him, "between shooting down a man who is trying to kill Garrison, and going out after a man who you know wants to kill him?"

Harlan grimaced. "I'll work that out," he said, "when I come to it."

Cole McAfee stood up and tossed his cigar out into the road. "Let me know when somebody's killed," he said sourly. "At least I can notify the coroner."

Harlan watched him go, and then took a cigar from his pocket and put it in his mouth. He found a wicker chair in the shadows at the far end of the porch and sat down, putting a match to the cigar.

He'd noticed that in the evening the smell was not so bad. Cooling breezes came down from the mountains to sweep away the sulphur fumes which were the price Rimrock had to pay for its millions in copper ore.

The streets were not too crowded now, because the night shift had not come out of the mines as yet, and the miners who were going on duty had not left their homes, or were having a quick one in Rimrock's thirty-two saloons before heading up to the shafts.

Across the road, out in front of the Montana Saloon, two miners were involved in a heated argument which in a matter of moments became physical. When they started punching each other, Cole McAfee angled quickly across the road, moved in between them, knocked one miner out into the road with his shoulder,

56

and smashed the other back against a wooden awning upright, holding him there until he cooled off.

The fight was over even before a crowd could gather, and there weren't more than a half-dozen people in town who'd known that it was going on.

Harlan puffed on his cigar and watched McAfee talking with the two miners, and then they nodded gruffly to each other and went in opposite directions. Cole McAfee adjusted his belt, straightened his black, flat-brimmed hat, and had a look in over the doors of the Montana Saloon before passing on, making his rounds of the town.

Cole McAfee was the ideal lawman. He liked his work, and he liked an orderly town. Here he was working in the most corrupt town in the West, a town which could blow up any moment, as he'd admitted himself.

Four men rode by from the direction of the mines, and Harlan recognized the man in the lead as the broad-shouldered Griff Morgan. Morgan didn't see him sitting back in the shadows.

After a while Harlan finished the cigar and went upstairs to his room which adjoined Boyd Garrison's. He saw the light under the door of Garrison's room as he went by, and he heard the hum of conversation. He wondered what could have caused this meeting with Garrison's surveyors on this particular night, the night that a party was being held to celebrate Judge Brynn's election to office.

The celebration party had ended shortly after Garrison had departed for the High Dollar Mine, and

Harlan found himself wondering who had escorted Miss Brynn home. Garrison himself didn't seem to be too concerned about it. His midnight meeting with his surveyors evidently was of greater importance.

Long after he'd gone to bed Harlan could still hear them talking in low voices in the other room, and he judged there were at least four or five men in the room. Boyd Garrison was undoubtedly preparing for another big killing.

Garrison knocked on the door and came in early the next morning as Harlan was shaving. He looked trim and fresh despite the fact that he'd been up late the previous evening.

Harlan said, "Need me?"

"Going up to the hill," Garrison told him. "Thought you might like to be in on it."

He was grinning boyishly as he spoke, and Harlan stared at him in the mirror as he wielded the razor.

"In on what?" he asked.

"We're hitting William Andrews the biggest blow he's ever received since coming to Montana." Garrison chuckled.

"Below the belt?" Harlan murmured.

Garrison's grin departed. "I wish you hadn't said that, Craig," he said. "I like you, and I want to continue liking you."

"It was out of line," Harlan admitted. "I'll take it back."

"You know and I know," Garrison continued, "that in this business there are no illegal blows. If I hadn't played the same game the other operators are playing in this territory, I'd be working for three dollars a day down in the mines."

Harlan finished shaving and washed the lather from his face. Turning around, he said, "I'll go along whether it's part of my job or not. I'm a curious man."

"This is something even Andrews never thought of." Garrison grinned. "He's claiming we're taking ore out of his Bengal Tiger Mine. Now we'll start taking ore out of our own shaft, but he'll like that even less."

Harlan noticed as they went downstairs to the hotel dining room that Garrison didn't tell him what his plan was. A man never showed his cards in this town until he played them.

As they came down into the lobby Harlan saw Marcia Reynolds coming in from the street, a package under her arm. As she was walking toward the desk she saw Harlan and nodded, giving him a faint smile.

Boyd Garrison saw her, too, and Harlan noticed that he slowed down.

"You know her?" he asked Harlan softly as they were crossing the lobby.

"Met her in Barnhouse's office," Harlan explained. "Runs a dress shop in town for the fashionable ladies."

"Ask her in for a cup of coffee," Garrison urged.

Harlan looked at him. "If I ask her," he said, "it wouldn't be for you."

Garrison grinned. "If that's how it is, all right, but ask her anyway. I'm curious."

Harlan wondered where Julia Brynn fitted into this picture. He noticed that Miss Reynolds was speaking with the clerk at the desk, apparently inquiring about a customer to whom she was delivering a dress. She had half-turned, however, and she was looking in their direction.

As she moved away from the desk and started toward the stairs which led to the second floor, Harlan left Garrison and met her halfway. He touched his hat, and said:

"Mr. Garrison and I would like you to join us for a cup of coffee in the dining room, Miss Reynolds."

He saw her turquoise eyes flick, and she glanced past him at Garrison still standing in the doorway, hat in hand. This morning she was wearing a green velvet jacket which brought out the color of her hair. Her hat was of the same material with a bright orange feather in it.

She said softly, "I've wanted to meet Mr. Garrison, Mr. Craig."

Harlan frowned. "Reckon that wasn't the idea," he said, "but we'd still like to have you, ma'am."

"I have a dress to deliver upstairs." She smiled. "Can I meet you in ten minutes?"

"We'll have a table," Harlan told her.

He went back to Garrison and said briefly, "She's coming later."

"Good." Garrison nodded. "How long you say she's been in town?"

"Not long," Harlan said.

They took a corner table and sat down, and Garrison touched a match to a cigar.

"It's strange I haven't seen her before," he said.

60

"You've been too busy making money," Harlan told him.

"You have a point." Garrison grinned.

They had a breakfast of bacon and eggs, and were drinking their coffee when Marcia Reynolds joined them.

Garrison was up on his feet immediately, offering her a chair, and Harlan noticed that she sat down next to him at the table.

"This is very kind of you," she said, after Harlan had made the introductions.

"Which one of us?" Harlan asked.

Both of them laughed, and Harlan, glancing at them, had the feeling that they were well-matched, and this knowledge didn't put him in any better mood.

"I have heard a great deal about you, Mr. Garrison," Marcia was saying. "You have a big reputation back in Chicago."

Garrison smiled. "I hope all that you've heard is good?"

"They say you've been giving the trusts a hard time," Marcia told him. "Is that good?"

"If you're not associated with United Copper it is." Garrison smiled, evidently pleased with the remark.

He asked her questions concerning her business and her customers, and Harlan knew that he was going to see to it that plenty of business was turned her way.

Harlan sipped his coffee and said very little, resentment building up inside of him. Garrison seemed in no hurry to finish his chat with Miss Reynolds and get on with his business. Harlan was positive he would have stayed there indefinitely if a boy hadn't come in with a message that the buckboard he was renting for the morning was waiting outside.

They saw Miss Reynolds to the door, and then both men stepped into the buckboard.

"A very attractive young lady," Garrison murmured. "I commend you on your taste, Harlan."

"I could say the same for you," Harlan retorted, "in more instances than one."

Boyd Garrison laughed heartily and clapped Harlan on the back before he drove the buckboard up the street and out of town.

They met three of his surveyors up at the shaft of the High Dollar Mine where they had been waiting patiently, and as they were stepping out of the buckboard, Ed Nicholson, the mine superintendent, came up in a gig driven by Cole McAfee.

Harlan looked at the sheriff curiously, wondering what was bringing him up here early in the morning.

Nicholson said briefly to Garrison, "We're closed down for the time being, Mr. Garrison. United Copper has brought an injunction against us to close the High Dollar shaft until the court decides whether or not we are encroaching on Bengal Tiger territory."

Garrison looked at Cole McAfee. "That right?" he asked.

McAfee yawned. "I have orders to close the High Dollar. You'll do me a favor by not causing me any trouble."

"I never tangle with the law," Garrison said.

"I know." McAfee smiled grimly. "You have other ways."

"Get the crew out of the mine," Garrison said to his superintendent, "and then go back to town and instruct Mr. Gillette that we want a court order to close the Bengal Tiger, inasmuch as they have just broken into a stope of the High Dollar and have been in armed conflict with my crew."

Harlan saw Cole McAfee's mouth tighten slightly. "You realize, Mr. Garrison," he said slowly, "that this will throw two thousand men out of work in this town?"

Garrison shrugged. "It will not be long," he stated. To Nicholson he said, "Pass the word to our miners as they are laid off that it is because of a court order instituted by William Andrews."

"You never miss a trick," McAfee said. "I might as well head over to the Bengal Tiger and wait for my instructions from Judge Brynn."

"Do you blame me?" Garrison asked him.

"No." McAfee scowled. "Around here it's a case of dog eat dog, and the devil with the man who's caught in between."

Harlan watched him ride on in the gig, and then he sat down on a pile of timbers nearby and touched a match to a cigar. Nicholson went into the shafthouse and spoke with one of his mine bosses. Later, he rode back to town on a saddle horse he took from a shed farther up the hill.

While Garrison was having his conference with his surveyors, the miners started coming out of the cage as it was lowered and raised, and then lowered again.

They blinked into the bright light as they came out, pasty-faced, sweaty, dirty, sullen because they were being laid off. Their resentment was against William Andrews and United Copper. Several of them cursed Andrews openly as they trudged past the spot where Harlan sat.

There were several hundred men down in the High Dollar, working on the morning shift, and less than a hundred of them had come up out of the shaft when Fred Barnhouse arrived in a buckboard.

The newspaper man looked at Harlan and frowned. "More trouble," he said. "I just passed Nicholson going in. So Garrison is having the Bengal Tiger closed, too."

"That's it." Harlan nodded. "A heck of a business."

"The two biggest mines on the lode," Barnhouse muttered. "That means two thousand men hanging around the saloons in Rimrock with nothing to do, and both groups blaming the other for being laid off. You know what can happen, don't you, Craig?"

"They can blow the lid off this town," Harlan said, "when they get enough drink in them, and they've sat around long enough for the novelty to wear off." He puffed on the cigar. "What happens in court now?"

"A hearing will be held," Barnhouse told him. "Judge Brynn will hear witnesses. Supposedly impartial surveyors and mining engineers will be called in to give testimony. Both staffs of lawyers will hack at each other, and then Judge Brynn will give his decision."

"If he opens one mine and doesn't open the other," Harlan said, "there'll be the devil to pay."

Barnhouse didn't say anything to that. He was watching Garrison's surveyors, who had gone up beyond the shaft of the High Dollar and were setting up their instruments.

"What's going on here?" he asked.

"Garrison's big secret," Harlan observed. "He's been acting like a little boy this morning, waiting for Christmas."

Barnhouse shrugged. "Routine survey of his claim, I suppose," he said. "He couldn't be staking out a new claim, because every foot of the hill was grabbed ten years ago."

Garrison came over and sat down next to Harlan, getting a light for his cigar from Harlan's. He said to Barnhouse:

"Better hold up your paper today, Fred. Might be some big news coming in before noon."

"Already got the news," Barnhouse observed. "William Andrews got out a court injection closing the High Dollar, and you're getting out another to close the Bengal Tiger."

"Put that on the second page." Garrison smiled through the cigar smoke.

Fred Barnhouse turned to look at him, his jaw drooping a little.

"You've got something bigger?" he asked.

"When my surveyors are finished," Garrison chuckled, "I'll let you know."

Barnhouse shrugged. "Your surveyors will try to prove in court that United Copper is digging ore out of your High Dollar Mine, and United Copper will try to prove that you're digging ore out of their Bengal Tiger. That's not news, Garrison."

"And that's only a guess you're making about my news," Garrison grinned, "and it's all wrong."

Barnhouse looked at him thoughtfully. Miners were still coming up out of the High Dollar, moving past them down the hill toward town. A dozen of them piled into an ore wagon and went careening down toward the main street, having already had a few drinks before they came up out of the mine.

"I'll hold up the paper," Barnhouse said, "if you've got the news, Garrison."

"This will be the biggest thing to hit Rimrock since the news of the outbreak of the Civil War." Garrison laughed. "It'll be worth waiting for."

For some time they watched the surveyors moving about on the east slope of the hill above the High Dollar shaft.

"They've made a survey of the entire hill since last week," Garrison explained. "This morning we are finishing up, and by nightfall William Andrews and every other operator on the lode will be shaking in his boots."

"I want to see that," Barnhouse told him.

Harlan sat on the pile of lumber in the bright morning sunshine. Boyd Garrison had taken off his hat, and the sun glinted on his hair, making it bronze in color. He was the handsome god of this hill just as Marcia Reynolds, with similar coloring, could be looked upon as the goddess of Rimrock. They both had copper in them.

Looking at Garrison, Harlan again felt resentment.

66

CHAPTER
SEVEN

It was past noon when the surveyors completed their work, and Harlan watched them knock a few wooden stakes into the ground two hundred yards above the High Dollar shaft. The area of ground covered by the stakes did not amount to more than two hundred square feet, and formed a kind of lopsided triangle.

Barnhouse had returned to town, and Harlan remained with Boyd Garrison on the hill, watching curiously as the men drove in the stakes.

"I'm not a mining man," Harlan observed, "but if I were I'd say that you were staking out a claim here, Garrison."

"You are very observing," Garrison grinned. "Now we'll go down to the claim office in town."

Harlan stared at him. "Then you are staking out a claim?"

"These men," Garrison told him, "are the best surveyors in Rimrock. I've been paying them big money for a week. It wasn't just to have them drive a few sticks of wood into the ground. We are staking out a claim on the hill."

"Barnhouse said that every foot of land on the hill had been staked out at least ten years ago."

Garrison shrugged. "According to my surveyors," he said laughingly, "Barnhouse was wrong." He nodded toward the new stakes in the barren ground. "That section has never been taken. We've checked every claim in the claim office. We've gone over survey maps of the hill. This little triangle lies between my High Dollar, the Bengal Tiger, and two other mines on the hill."

Harlan looked at the stakes uncomprehendingly. "You mean you're going to mine copper out of that?" he said incredulously. "You couldn't even put a shaft up there. It's too small."

"There is no law," Garrison grinned, "which says that a mining claim must fit any particular measurement. The law only restricts one man from laying claim to too much territory. If I want to claim a small section such as this, the law cannot stop me."

"It's legal," Harlan scowled, "but how honest is it?"

The smile left Garrison's smooth-shaven face. He said slowly, "You're new to this town, Harlan, and this seems to you like a dishonest move. Did anybody ever tell you how William Andrews got possession of the Bengal Tiger and the Whistle Stop Mine on the hill?"

"No," Harlan said.

"The Bengal Tiger," Garrison grated, "one of the richest producers on the lode; was stolen from poor Pat Buchanan, an ignorant Irishman with a thirst for strong liquor. Andrews' engineers certified to him that the Bengal Tiger was worth millions, how many millions we don't even know now because it's still one of the big producers with no end in sight. Buchanan didn't know

68

that, and Buchanan's lawyers convinced him that five thousand was a good price for his claim. They had to get him good and drunk, though, before he would sign his name to a paper."

Harlan kicked at one of the wooden sticks and said nothing.

"The Whistle Stop," Garrison went on tersely, "on the north slope of the hill; was stolen from Jack Wilson's widow. Jack himself was found knifed in an alley behind the Paradise Saloon one night. Two days before, he'd turned down all of William Andrews' offers to buy the Whistle Stop, because he knew his claim was worth a fortune as soon as he could borrow money and start mining on a large scale. His widow sold out for three thousand. She had five children to support, and no source of income."

"All right," Harlan murmured. He was looking down the hill toward town.

"What happened to me," Garrison said, "when I was making a speech against United Copper candidates before the election? What happened to you when you intervened to save my life? We're not playing for marbles up here, Harlan. I've discovered that there's only one way to fight men like William Andrews. You fight their kind of fight, and you hit them first."

"It's your conscience," Harlan told him. "You have to live with it."

"And so far," Garrison smiled, his good humor returning, "I have had no difficulty." He put a hand on Harlan's shoulder. "Let's go down and file this claim."

As they were riding down the grade in the buckboard Harlan said to him, "You think Andrews will let you get away with this?"

"He'll fight," Garrison answered, "and I'll fight him back, and he'll know that he's in a fight."

They hailed Fred Barnhouse just coming out of the office of the *Miner*, and Garrison said:

"Meet us at the claim office, Fred, if you want your story."

"The claim office?" Barnhouse repeated, puzzled.

"That's the story," Garrison told him, and moved the buckboard down the street.

Already the town was full of miners who'd come out of the High Dollar, and very shortly, Harlan knew, they would be coming down from the Bengal Tiger, too, when the court injunction went into effect. Groups of men stood on the corners and on the porches of saloons, discussing the situation.

When the Bengal Tiger miners started to troop down from the hill there could easily be trouble as long as the liquor held out. Harlan mentioned this fact to Garrison, and the mine operator said casually:

"McAfee's job to maintain order in Rimrock."

As they were passing the Montana Saloon, Griff Morgan, who had been standing with a group of men, turned to look at them. He had a half-smoked cigar in his mouth, and as the buckboard rolled by he tossed the cigar at one of the wheels. His pale green eyes were hard and tough as he sized up both men.

Garrison said as they went by, "When are you going to fight him, Harlan?"

Harlan smiled faintly. "Must I?" he asked.

Garrison shrugged. "You've had words," he stated. "Everything starts with words, but I don't think Morgan will let it stop there."

"Would you fight him?" Harlan asked, staring at the horse's ears up ahead.

"Only if I had to." Garrison chuckled. "He's a rough one, and he'd probably kill me. I think you'd give him a tussle."

"And you'd like to see that."

"I'm not egging you on," Garrison told him. "You're working for me. It's not part of your job to go after Griff Morgan unless you have trouble with him on your own."

He drove the buckboard up to the claim office on the next block, and stepped down from the seat. Harlan remained where he was, turning his head to watch Fred Barnhouse coming down, his long legs moving rapidly.

"You'll stay here?" Garrison asked, and Harlan nodded.

Garrison lifted a hand to Fred Barnhouse, and then went into the building. Watching him, Harlan wondered if the man were signing his death warrant. If so, he was going about it very coolly.

Barnhouse came up breathlessly and put one hand on the buckboard seat as he spoke.

"He's not filing a claim?" he panted.

"That's it," Harlan told him.

"He can't!"

"You go in and tell him that." Harlan smiled. "He has a little triangle up above the High Dollar which he claims was never taken up by anyone, according to his surveyors and engineers. It's a little wedge, large enough for a pea patch. He claims he can take copper out of it."

Barnhouse was staring at him, a stunned expression still on his face.

"I know what he's doing," he said finally. "I know what he has in mind."

"He's mining copper," Harlan said, "and the devil with William Andrews and everyone else."

"It's more than that," Barnhouse muttered. "He's after all of it; he's out for the whole hill."

"From that pea patch?" Harlan asked him, smiling a little.

"According to the mining law," Barnhouse said slowly, "as it pertains to silver and copper, a mine operator is entitled to follow a vein of metal no matter where it leads if the vein begins on his claim. This is called the Apex theory, and it has produced countless lawsuits in Rimrock and in every mining town in America. This little pea patch, as you call it, upon which Garrison is filing, contains copper ore. He can go down, and then follow whatever ore veins he pleases, no matter where they go, right through the Bengal Tiger, or any other mine on the lode. All he has to do is claim that he's hit the mother lode on this little patch of ground."

"Can he get away with that?" Harlan asked.

"With a good staff of lawyers, engineers and geologists, and some influence in the local court,"

Barnhouse murmured, "he might get away with almost anything in this town."

Harlan could see now the importance of Garrison putting his own man on the bench in Rimrock. Undoubtedly Garrison had had this coup in mind for a long time. Now he was going to work at it.

"Suppose he has hit the mother lode up there between his stakes?" Harlan asked curiously. "Is that possible?"

Barnhouse laughed. "Who can tell which is the lead vein?" he pointed out. "Below the surface ore veins are broken up. You follow one and it peters out, only to begin again ten feet farther on. Is that the same vein, or a new one? Who can prove it?"

"The man with the most guns behind him," Harlan murmured.

"So watch the trains from now on," Barnhouse told him grimly. "You'll see them coming off in droves — the hired gunhands of United Copper, and also of Boyd Garrison. This town will become an armed camp before it's finished, with these two injunctions throwing men out of work, and now Garrison trying to drive United Copper off the hill."

A few minutes later Garrison came out of the claim office, smiling broadly. He said to Barnhouse:

"We've hit the mother lode up on the hill, Fred."

"I know," Barnhouse said gloomily.

"Will you print that?"

Barnhouse shrugged. "It's news," he said. "I print the news. You won't get away with it, though, Garrison. You know that."

"I can try." Garrison looked past Harlan, who had gotten off the buckboard to talk with Barnhouse, and when Harlan turned his head slightly, he saw Griff Morgan coming up, a crowd following him.

Griff had a peculiar rolling walk, and there was a glint in his eyes which Harlan understood very well. Griff had decided this was the time.

Fred Barnhouse saw them coming up, and said, "Everything happens at once."

Griff addressed himself to Boyd Garrison first, even though he was sizing Harlan up. He said, "You boys had your little fun last night underground. Now we're out in the sunlight where I can see you."

"Take a good look." Garrison chuckled.

"What would you do, Mr. Garrison," Griff asked him, "if I were to throw you down in the dirt now and stamp on you?"

"I would shoot you dead first," Garrison told him, "and then sue you for assault and battery."

"You would not fight me with your hands?" Griff asked softly.

Garrison looked him over carefully. He was the taller man, but Morgan was considerably heavier, with his barrel chest, thick neck and solid, heavy legs.

"I would not fight you with my hands." Garrison agreed pleasantly. "I have never cared for rolling in the dirt."

"And what about your boy here?" Griff asked him, nodding toward Harlan, but not looking at him.

"My associate," Garrison told him, "can speak for himself."

74

The little crowd around the buckboard was swelling already as the word passed through the street that Griff Morgan was pushing a fight. Harlan saw them hurrying down from saloons, crowding in around them on the walk and in the road.

"What is it you want?" Harlan asked, no emotion in his voice.

"You were down in the High Dollar last night?" Griff asked him, turning for the first time to face him directly.

Harlan nodded. "That's right."

"Throwing lead at my boys from behind a rock?"

"Spitting at them," Harlan said.

Someone laughed in the crowd, and Griff's face twitched, his green eyes receding into his head.

"You came to this town," he said, "with a big mouth, Craig. I'd like to change the shape of that mouth."

"Now?" Harlan asked.

"Now."

Harlan started to take off his coat, and Boyd Garrison said laughingly, "You whip this man, and I'll double your salary, Harlan."

"Don't bother," Harlan said. "I'll whip him for my own pleasure."

He draped his coat over the buckboard seat as Griff Morgan started to take off his coat, and then he turned and pushed through the crowd and out into the middle of the road. As he did so he saw Marcia Reynolds come out of a store on the other side of the street.

She saw him in the street and stopped, seeing the crowd, hearing the noise which was beginning to build

75

up. A man was yelling in over the bat-wing doors of a nearby saloon:

"Griff Morgan's got one! Come an' see it, gents."

Harlan frowned at the girl on the walk, and motioned for her to walk on. She took a few steps and stopped, and then she stood there, watching.

Harlan had no more time for her, because Griff Morgan was coming out in to the road, and the crowd was beginning to yell.

"You still got time to run, Jack," Griff grinned, "and it's only three blocks to the railroad station."

"You came here to fight," Harlan told him. "Stop the talk."

Griff Morgan moved in with pile-driver blows, moving faster than Harlan had thought he could. He was a short, powerful bear, tearing with both claws, and for the moment Harlan backed away, knowing that if Griff were able to catch him with one solid blow it might mean a quick finish to the fight.

He retreated into the crowd, defending himself as best he could, taking a few glancing blows on the face and the arms. Griff's knuckles cut his right cheek, and he felt the blood begin to drip down his chin, but he was not hurt.

He circled, watching carefully, and then when Griff's attack subsided, he leaped in fast, lashing out with his right fist, catching Morgan flush on the nose. He heard the bones crackle in Griff's nose, and a quick cry of pain leap from Griff's mouth.

Blood gushed from the broken nose, and Griff stood in his tracks for a moment, too shocked to move. He recovered very quickly, however, and roared in, blood dripping down across his white shirt front.

Harlan was waiting for him this time, and landed several solid blows to the body before Griff Morgan's superior weight drove him back. He'd expected Griff to be soft in the body because the mine superintendent was not doing manual labor in the mines, but here he was mistaken. His fists bounced off the squat man's body, and he knew that he was in for a fight.

"You're rough," Griff panted, "and I like it better that way. It'll last longer."

"Save your breath," Harlan advised.

He was ready for Griff's next drive, and as the short man came in, he stepped aside and chopped him hard with his right fist. Griff lost his balance and pitched forward into the dust of the road.

There was a moment's respite as Griff got to his feet again without any particular haste, and apparently little hurt.

Harlan had a chance to look around, and noticed that Boyd Garrison had joined Miss Reynolds over on the walk across the road. They were both watching, and Harlan was not particularly pleased. The fight would not be pretty to watch, and he wondered why Garrison didn't insist upon the girl's leaving.

"We'll dance around again," Griff Morgan was saying. "You twirl me and I'll twirl you, Craig."

Harlan wondered what it was going to take to hurt this man. He'd hit him a number of savage blows to the body and to the head, and Griff's senses were still as clear as when he'd started to fight. With the blood still dripping from his battered nose, he was as confident as ever that he could whip this man.

Apparently Griff's plan of battle was to wear his man down, and then batter him unmercifully when he was too weak to keep out of the way. He would take a dreadful beating himself this way, but the beating the other man would take from then on was not pleasant to think about.

Harlan waited for him to come in, deciding that he too would conserve his strength rather than risk breaking his hands on Griff's hard head.

He noticed that the crowd was still gathering, drawn from the other ends of town. There were several hundred people watching the fight from various vantage points, and it was not a particularly noisy crowd. It was as if they knew it was going to be a long dog-fight, and were settling back to watch.

Fred Barnhouse was sitting up on the seat of the buckboard nearby, watching without any particular enthusiasm. He'd evidently seen Griff fight before, and he was not hopeful of Harlan's chances.

Harlan circled and hit, and avoided Griff's patient rushes, and then hit again. He ripped the flesh on Griff's right cheek, and cut him over the right eye, and then Griff landed solidly for the first time since the fight had begun.

Harlan saw the blow coming, an overhand right, and he pulled away to avoid it, but as he did so Griff caught him with a left to the body, and Harlan went down, gasping for air.

As he rolled Griff went at him, kicking hard with his right boot at Harlan's face. Harlan managed to move his face away, avoiding the full force of the blow, but Griff was aiming another, and this one would have smashed bones in his face if it had landed.

It didn't land, however, because Boyd Garrison had torn through the crowd like a wild man, coming up behind Griff. He hit the shorter man like a battering ram, sending him reeling into the buckboard and making it shake.

The crowd whooped, "Give it to him, Mr. Garrison."

Harlan got to his feet, rubbed his stomach, and looked at Boyd Garrison curiously. Garrison was standing in front of him, giving him time to get up before Griff could get at him again.

Griff came away from the buckboard, his face a bloody mask, and grinning. He said, "You like some of this, too, Mr. Garrison?"

"Come with a gun," Garrison told him, "any time you wish."

"All right," Harlan said. "I am obliged, Mr. Garrison."

"I don't like to see a man kicked," Garrison growled. "You're a gutter fighter, Morgan."

"I aim to whip a man," Griff said. "I don't care how."

Garrison stepped away, and Griff came at Harlan again. He was confident now, and very strong. Watching him, Harlan knew that he'd have to end it quickly if at all because Griff would certainly wear him down in time.

When Griff charged, instead of retreating, he moved straight toward his man, meeting him with a flurry of hard, punishing blows which drove Griff back against the buckboard.

The crowd started to yell as Harlan pinned his man against the rear wheel of the buckboard, and kept hitting with all his strength, never giving Griff a chance to get set and fight back. He struck at Griff's face and at his body, slogging blows which sounded like rocks striking mud.

He used up all of his strength in this last desperate drive with the knowledge that if Griff got away from him now, and was able to recover, he himself would be finished.

Griff's eyes were puffy, cut, and now they became slightly glazed as Harlan struck at him. He mumbled and tried to get away from the buckboard, but Harlan wouldn't let him go. And then Griff started to slide down the wheel. He landed in a sitting position in the dust of the road, his face unrecognizable, and Harlan turned away, his arms limp at his sides, breathing agonizingly.

He managed to reach the boardwalk, and he sat down on the edge of it, where Boyd Garrison joined him. The big crowd still filling the street was cheering him, and Garrison said: "You've made a lot of friends here this afternoon, Harlan."

And an enemy, Harlan thought, *who'll have no rest until I'm dead, or he is.*

CHAPTER
EIGHT

Boyd Garrison and Fred Barnhouse got Harlan back to his room at the hotel. He was bleeding from several cuts on his face, and his left eye was swelling badly.

"Feel all right?" Garrison asked him.

"I'll live." Harlan smiled wryly. "How is Griff?"

"He's not pretty to look at," Barnhouse stated as he poured water into a porcelain basin. "What did it get you, Craig?"

"His fight," Harlan observed. "He wanted it."

They washed the blood from his face, and he held a wet compress to his swollen eye. Barnhouse went down to bring up a bottle of brandy, and Boyd Garrison sat down on the edge of a chair across the room, looking at Harlan curiously.

"I didn't think you'd whip him," he said finally. "You're tougher than I thought you were, Harlan."

"If you hadn't stepped in when he had me down," Harlan said, "it would have been the other way around."

Garrison shrugged. "He'd kill me in a fight," he said, "but I couldn't see him stomping on you."

Barnhouse came back with the brandy and a few glasses, and when Harlan had taken a mouthful he felt some of his strength returning.

"Now," Barnhouse said to Garrison, "we'll talk about this claim you staked on the hill. You're sure it's clear, and I can print that?"

"Survey map in the claim office proves that no one has filed on that little patch," Garrison told him.

"And you're going to mine copper ore there." Barnhouse scowled.

"The mother lode." Garrison grinned. "We're digging down, and we're following the lead vein even if it goes to the state of California."

"Your engineers claim it's the apex of the mother lode?" Barnhouse asked.

"My staff of engineers have come to that conclusion," Garrison chuckled, "which fact they will testify to in court."

"Then you'll start mining copper ore," Barnhouse said slowly, "under, above, and through any other claims on the hill. Is that right?"

"A mine operator would be a fool not to follow the lead vein," Garrison told him, "after he'd located it and staked out legal claim."

Barnhouse nodded, and then he pointed a finger at Harlan, sitting on the edge of the bed, holding the wet towel to his face. He said, "You see that man, Mr. Garrison?"

"I do." Garrison nodded, humor in his hazel eyes.

"You'll need fifty more like him," Barnhouse said tersely, "if you expect to take ore out of that patch upon which you've just filed."

"If I need them," Garrison told him, "I'll get them."

Fred Barnhouse just shook his head and went out.

Harlan said from the bed, "You're making this a rough town, Mr. Garrison."

"It was rough before I came here," Garrison scowled, "and dirty, and no low blows barred. William Andrews and men like him made it that way, and they're millionaires. I came along later, but I'll get my share."

"You want the whole hill?" Harlan asked him.

Boyd Garrison poured himself a glass of the brandy and held it up to the light. He said slowly, "Do you know what it is to be poor and respectable, Harlan?"

"I've been broke," Harlan stated.

"That's one thing," Garrison told him, "but it is not too bad. When your pockets are empty, and you have to be respectable, that's something else. I came from a home like that, a respectable home in Illinois, where the family had to keep up pretenses even though it might mean going without food. My father was a schoolteacher, a debt-ridden one, with five children and a small salary. We were decent people, but I learned there what it meant to squeeze pennies. I saw what it did to my father and my mother. It'll not happen to me."

"You're way ahead now," Harlan observed. "You wouldn't need any more."

Garrison laughed. "You're not wise in the ways of high finance, Harlan," he said. "In this business you're tied up. My money is invested in copper ore smelters, in mining machinery, in a few claims on the hill. If William Andrews were to throw a wrench into the machinery, I might be back on the ash heap in less than a month. This is a cat fight in Rimrock. A man is a millionaire today, and he's broke tomorrow. I've seen it happen. Supposing Judge Brynn were to uphold Andrews' injunction and throw mine out of the window? Where would I be?"

"Any chance of that?" Harlan smiled.

"Who knows what chance there is of anything?" Garrison muttered, and for once Harlan saw the other man in him — the young man who had come out of an Illinois town with empty pockets, fearful, but resolved that he would never again lack for money.

Garrison downed his drink, and walked to the window to look down on the street. He said over his shoulder, "You know where you stand in Rimrock now, Harlan. You're an enemy of United Copper, and you know their tactics. You can still pull out of here if you want to before you end up in an alley with a bullet through the back of your head."

"Reckon I'll stay," Harlan said.

"Why?"

Harlan looked at him around the towel. He'd turned from the window again, and was looking at Harlan quizzically.

"Maybe I'm getting to like this town," Harlan said.

There were two other reasons. One was Marcia Reynolds, who had been quite friendly, and the other was Julia Brynn, who was gentle and warm and kind, and who did not appear to be receiving a fair shake from Boyd Garrison.

"It might be a little rough for both you and I from now on," Garrison was saying. "I don't mind saying that I'm going to need you around, Harlan, even more than I thought I would."

84

"I'll stay," Harlan said. He was remembering how Garrison had jumped into this fight with Griff Morgan. "I don't like the job, but I'll stay."

There was a knock on the door, and when Garrison opened it, a boy announced that Mr. William Andrews was waiting down below, and wanted to see Mr. Garrison.

"Tell him to come right up," Garrison said, and when he'd closed the door he turned and grinned at Harlan. "I thought it would take less than ten minutes before Mr. Andrews learned of my visit to the claim office. You're going to meet the big wolf of Rimrock, Harlan. Come into my quarters."

Harlan followed him into the other suite. He'd been in the rooms before. They were ornately furnished with red plush, horse-hair chairs and sofas, and deep green carpeting on the floor. The lamps were the best to be had in the shops of 'Frisco. There were several paintings on the walls, and in one corner of the room a huge, mahogany roll-top desk.

Garrison maintained an office down on the street, but he received many visitors in his own quarters at the Empire.

"Why do you want me in on this?" Harlan asked him as he took a seat in a corner of the room.

"Like you to know what kind of man we're dealing with," Garrison told him. "You haven't met Mr. Andrews?"

"No," Harlan said.

"He doesn't look it," Garrison mused. "He doesn't look it at all. Griff Morgan could break him in pieces with his hands, but he's stronger and tougher and ten times more ruthless than Griff, and he won't fight you out in the open the way Griff will."

Harlan sat on the red plush chair, still holding the wet compress to his face. He said thoughtfully, "You have a staff of lawyers working for you, and big mine operators, and you want me to meet Mr. Andrews. I'm hired as your bodyguard for a salary. Why do you do this?"

Garrison smiled at him. "I'm a big man in this town," he stated, "and a fairly rich one. I know a great many people. There are very few I can't buy. I couldn't buy you, and therefore I trust you, Harlan. A man likes a friend even if he's rich."

Harlan looked down at the floor. "I'm obliged," he said.

There was a knock on the door then, and Mr. Andrews came in. Harlan had seen him on the street, but never at close range, and he studied the little man carefully.

Andrews was small, almost fragile, like a piece of rare china. His features were small, dainty and expressionless; he had a thin, high-boned face with a narrow, arching nose and deep-set gray eyes. He held his hat in his hand, a gray derby, and his hair was thin and gray. He said in soft, well-modulated tones, glancing in Harlan's direction:

"I was under the impression that we would be alone, Mr. Garrison."

"Harlan Craig, my bodyguard." Garrison smiled. "Meet Mr. Andrews of United Copper."

Harlan nodded without getting up, knowing that Andrews did not want to shake hands with him.

"I know who he is," Andrews purred, "and his relationship to you, Garrison."

"Mr. Craig is in my confidence," Garrison told him. "I prefer that he remain."

"I did not come here to kill you." Andrews smiled faintly.

"I didn't think you did," Garrison countered. "What can I do for you, Mr. Andrews?"

"Firstly," Andrews said flatly, "have that court order withdrawn closing up my Bengal Tiger Mine."

"You've closed me up," Garrison said, and he was no longer smiling.

"Secondly," William Andrews went on, almost in a monotone, "go back to the claim office and withdraw that claim you made this afternoon."

"What if I refuse on both counts?" Garrison asked him.

"You'll never take another pound of copper ore out of the hill," William Andrews told him quietly. "That's a promise, Garrison."

"That's a threat," Garrison snapped. "I am not impressed by threats, Mr. Andrews."

The big financier stood in the center of the room, looking at Garrison steadily for a few moments before he spoke again, and then he said slowly:

"I will break you, Mr. Garrison. If it takes every cent I've got, I will break you. If I have to ruin this town, I will break you."

Garrison was smiling, standing straight and tall near the window, and the sun was shining on his brown hair, making it coppery again. He was smiling, but there was no humor in him. It was a cold, grim smile.

"Make sure," he said, "that you do not ruin yourself, Mr. Andrews, in your attempts to break me."

"I will take every precaution," Mr. Andrews told him tersely. "As you know, I take very few chances, Mr. Garrison. Good day."

He went out, and Boyd Garrison closed the door behind him. Then, turning, he smiled broadly at Harlan.

"What do you think?" he asked.

"I wouldn't like to fight him," Harlan said.

"You're in it whether you like it or not," Garrison chuckled, "as long as you're on my side. We'll go down together if we go down."

"You'll go down harder than I will." Harlan smiled. "I was on the bottom when I hit this town."

He went back to his own room as Garrison sat down at his desk to look over some papers.

After a while, after looking in to see that Garrison was still working, Harlan drifted down into the lobby, and it was here that he met Julia Brynn. She was coming in from the street.

She stopped when she saw him, and he noticed that she was looking at his face closely.

"Are you all right, Mr. Craig?" she asked.

Harlan's eye was still swollen, but he'd cleaned himself up and changed his clothes, and he did not look too bad, except for the cuts.

"You heard about it?" he asked.

"News travels fast in this town," she said. "Did Morgan pick a fight with you?"

"Reckon he had to fight somebody after the Bengal Tiger was closed down." Harlan smiled. "I was his size."

"Now both mines are closed down," Julia said glumly, "and Father says there will surely be trouble in the streets."

"Stay off them at night," Harlan warned her. "Some of these men will be drinking all day. Toward night they'll get ugly."

The door behind Julia Brynn opened, and Marcia Reynolds came in. Again, she had a package under her arm, and she nodded to Harlan and said:

"Another dress fitting."

He noticed her looking at Julia with interest, and he said, "This is Miss Julia Brynn, Judge Brynn's daughter, Miss Reynolds."

"I've heard of your dress shop." Julia smiled. "I'll have to stop in some afternoon."

"I'll have tea for you," Marcia Reynolds nodded. "I've wanted to meet you, Miss Brynn."

Harlan had a good opportunity to compare the two. Marcia was slightly taller, and her hair was lighter in color, almost reddish compared to Julia's. She was more sure of herself, more poised, and if anything more beautiful, her features of the classic mold.

Looking at her, Harlan could see why Boyd Garrison had been attracted to her. He may have liked Julia Brynn, but Julia was a different type. She was sweet and innocent, and she would not have made the same impression on high New York or Chicago society as Marcia Reynolds.

"I see you did not come out of the fight too badly," Marcia was saying to Harlan. "For a while I was worried about you."

Harlan felt some color come to his face, and he saw the faint smile on Julia Brynn's face as she looked at him.

"It wasn't something I asked for," he said.

"You didn't run away from it, either." She smiled, and then she nodded to Julia Brynn and said, "I'd be pleased to have you stop in my shop, Miss Brynn."

She went on and up the stairs with her package.

Julia said, "She's a very beautiful girl."

Harlan nodded. "You don't see too many like her in this town," he stated. Then he added, "Nor like you, either, Miss Brynn."

"You are very kind," Julia said.

She went on up to her apartment at the hotel, and Harlan stepped outside just as Cole McAfee rode up and dismounted in front of the hotel. He was scowling as he confronted Harlan, and said:

"I ride up to close the Bengal Tiger Mine, and while I'm gone you have it out with Griff Morgan."

"He wanted it that way," Harlan said.

"You don't look too bad for it," McAfee observed. "He's a rough customer. Now what's this I hear about Garrison filing another claim up on the hill?"

"He filed a claim," Harlan said.

"What the devil is he trying to do?" McAfee exploded.

"Reckon you'll have to ask him," Harlan smiled. "My job is to keep him alive. Mining is his business."

"And your business will be pretty tough from now on," McAfee growled. "How long does he think he can stay alive stealing copper ore from United Copper?"

"He won't be stealing it," Harlan observed. "He thinks he's found the apex of the mother lode on the hill, and he's going to mine ore."

"Darned funny business," McAfee snapped. "One little patch of ground up on that hill never was claimed, and on that patch, big enough to bury a man in, Garrison says he's hit the mother lode. Who can ever prove where the mother lode is?"

"Garrison's mining engineers intend to prove it in court," Harlan told him.

"And after they prove it," McAfee growled, "what do you think will happen? You think William Andrews will say to Garrison, 'Take the whole hill'?"

"He already had his say." Harlan smiled. "He was in Garrison's apartment fifteen minutes ago."

"Then it's a war?"

"He threatened trouble," Harlan said.

"It would be a great blessing for this town," McAfee said tersely, "if both of them were run out, and honest mine operators permitted to take that ore out of the hill. Bengal Tiger miners are coming into town now, and you know what that means."

"Let them crack each other's skulls if that's what they want to do," Harlan said. "Nobody's pushing these fellows to take on a load and look for a fight."

"Fists I don't mind," McAfee told him, "but it never ends there. They used knives and guns, too, when it gets real rough, and the innocent get hurt."

Harlan shook his head. "Reckon I wouldn't care for your job, McAfee," he said. "How much help you have?"

"Three deputies," McAfee told him glumly, "to keep the peace."

Harlan looked up and down the long main street of Rimrock. More and more miners were coming down the hill, mingling with the crowds on the street, seeping into the saloons. A buckboard rattled by loaded with High Dollar miners, all of them drunk and yelling hilariously.

"They're happy today," McAfee said. "Wait a few days till they begin to feel the pinch. Then they get ugly, especially the ones with families. You can't tell kids there's a court order closing down the mine where the father works. You can't even tell a miner that. He knows there's ore in the hill, and it's his job to get it out. What the bigwigs are doing is none of his business. He wants to work; he wants his pay envelope each week."

Watching the buckboard go by, Harlan wondered if Boyd Garrison were justified in his fight with Andrews and United Copper. Andrews was a crook, but Garrison was making himself a bigger crook by fighting on Andrews' level.

CHAPTER
NINE

The first big fight of the mining war took place at eight o'clock in the evening of the day the two biggest mines were closed. Harlan watched it from a wicker chair on the porch of the Empire Hotel, a cigar in his mouth and his boots up on the rail.

The crowd spewed out of the Cheyenne Saloon directly across the way, and suddenly there were at least twelve men fighting in the dust of the road, and it was impossible to tell who was fighting whom.

Cole McAfee with his three deputies charged into the middle of it a few minutes after it had begun, and the four men wielding short, sawed-off clubs managed to separate the fighters and send them on their way. Two of the miners had to be half-carried back into the saloon for treatment.

At nightfall the night shifts from both mines were up and about, joining with the day crews. In drunken high spirits several groups of them had confiscated a few big ore wagons, and they were rolling up and down the street, whooping, waving whiskey bottles and holding red flares.

One wagon overturned on the next block, and Harlan could hear a man screaming as he was pinned under it. He was carried unconscious into the rear of the nearest saloon, and a doctor hurried down to the scene.

Ed Nicholson, the High Dollar Mine superintendent, had been up in Garrison's rooms having a conference with him, and both men came out on the porch after the wagon went over with a bang.

They stood a few feet away from where Harlan sat, and Garrison said grimly:

"That one of our wagons, Ed?"

"Darned if it's not." Nicholson scowled. "I'll dock those boys a week's pay for this."

"Get a padlock on the wagon yard," Garrison ordered, "and then have that wagon removed. Pass the word that the next man who takes High Dollar property from the premises without permission will be shot dead."

Nicholson moved off, and a short while later Harlan saw him with a dozen men, raising the wagon with the aid of ropes and jacks, and then hooking on the mules again. The wagon was rolled off in the direction of the High Dollar yard at the west end of town.

Boyd Garrison sat on the porch railing a few feet from Harlan, a frown on his face. There were other wagons still on the street, but they were not High Dollar wagons.

A group of miners lurching down the street came to a stop in front of the porch, seeing Garrison sitting there.

"When are we goin' back to work, Mr. Garrison?" one of them asked.

"United Copper closed us up," Garrison told them. "We can't open until the court clears us."

"Heck with the court," one man growled. "Never had no truck with judges an' lawyers. All crooks, every one of 'em."

When the miners walked on, Harlan said thoughtfully, "Pass it all over to United Copper."

"Don't think he's not passing it back to me," Garrison retorted. "Every one of his Bengal Tiger miners thinks I'm the devil with horns."

They sat on the porch and watched the crowd in the street getting wilder and wilder. It seemed that every ten minutes Cole McAfee and his band of deputies were charging in to break up a fight which threatened to become a free-for-all.

Once Julia Brynn came out on the porch, and both men stood up when she came through the door from the lobby of the hotel.

"What is happening, Boyd?" she asked. "I've never heard such noise in the street before."

"Better stay up in your rooms," Garrison advised. "This will be getting rougher all the time."

"I'm concerned about Father," Julia told him. "He went up to Windham this afternoon, and he hasn't returned yet."

"What is he doing up there?" Garrison asked, and he sounded almost peevish.

Harlan saw Julia glance at Garrison quickly.

"He went up to see Mark Caldwell. They're old friends."

Garrison didn't say anything to that.

"He rented a buckboard to drive up," Julia went on, "and he said he'd be home early in the evening. It's past nine o'clock now, isn't it?"

Garrison nodded, and turned to stare at the crowded street. There were still a few vehicles moving, one of them an ore wagon filled with miners, and a few girls from a dance hall nearby. They'd lashed a beer barrel to the tail gate of the wagon, and they were singing and shouting as they rode up and down, pausing to ladle out drinks to friends in the crowd.

Even as they watched a group of about a dozen men charge the wagon, which was a Bengal Tiger vehicle, the name emblazoned on the side, knocked the beer barrel from the tail gate and smashed it in with an axe.

As the Bengal Tiger miners clambered off the wagon, roaring with anger, the group which had caused the damage darted off into a nearby alley, yelling triumphantly.

The women left in the wagon screamed insults after the men who'd smashed the barrel.

Boyd Garrison said, "You'd better go up to your rooms, Julia. I'll watch for your father."

"You think there'll be trouble?" she asked worriedly.

"The Judge is respected," Garrison assured her. "Don't worry about it."

When she'd left Harlan said quietly, "How much respect does Judge Brynn have in this town, Garrison? You know perfectly well that if he rides a buckboard down the middle of this street they're liable to pull him off the seat and ride him on a rail."

"You don't think I'll let that happen, do you?" Garrison growled.

"You won't stop it," Harlan told him, "once it starts. Those Bengal Tiger men think Brynn is responsible for closing them out. If they catch sight of him he's in for it."

Garrison thought a moment, and then he threw away a half-smoked cigar.

"Brynn will be coming in from Windham on the old stage road entering Rimrock at the east end of town," he said. "Ride out and stop him. Bring him in through the back streets. I'll get Ed Nicholson and line up a squad of sober men in case there is trouble."

Harlan left immediately, going to the rear of the hotel and picking up a saddle horse. He rode down the main street at a hard gallop, hoping he wouldn't meet Judge Brynn's rig coming in.

Drunken miners cursed him as he hammered by, missing some of them narrowly as they lurched down the middle of the street. As he moved past the Paradise Saloon he saw Griff Morgan out in front, a white bandage across his broken nose.

Morgan turned to look after him as he went by, recognizing him in the light from one of the saloons.

Harlan kept going, riding hard up a grade leading out of town, and pausing on the summit to breathe the horse before starting down the other side. Behind him he could see the lights of Rimrock, and he could hear the noise faintly.

The night was cool and clear, and a crescent moon gleamed above the hills. Windham, a small mining town, lay a half-dozen miles to the east, and Judge Brynn's buckboard was undoubtedly on the road, heading in his direction.

Harlan let the horse run again. He'd picked out a good animal in the livery stable, a big chestnut with plenty of bottom, and the horse was well-rested.

They had covered about a mile or more when he saw the buckboard coming down a small grade, the rider up on the seat. He pulled off the road and waited for him.

When the buckboard came up he called, "Judge Brynn?"

"Who is this?" Brynn asked suspiciously.

"Harlan Craig," Harlan told him, riding up. "Mr. Garrison sent me out to stop you."

"Trouble in town?" Brynn asked. He was smoking a cigar, and Harlan could see the dull glow of the butt end in his mouth.

"Rimrock's full of drunken miners," Harlan explained. "You ride in on the main street with this buckboard, and there might be trouble. Garrison suggests we come in through a side street to the hotel."

Judge Brynn said softly, "Mr. Garrison is quite concerned about my safety, Craig. I'll do as you say."

There was a note of irony in his voice, and Harlan couldn't get it out of his mind that Otis Brynn had very little use for Boyd Garrison.

"You want to ride with me and tie your horse to the tailgate," Brynn asked, "or would it be safer to ride on ahead and clear the way?"

"I'll move up ahead," Harlan said. "You know your way to the hotel through some of the back streets?"

"There is a back road which leads around the Wyandotte Mine and approached the town from the north side," Judge Brynn told him. "I'll turn off there. The road is another half-mile or so up ahead."

Harlan lifted a hand to him and started back along the road he'd come. He heard the buckboard wheels start to move, and then he heard something else in the direction of Rimrock — the pounding hoofs of fast-moving horses.

For one moment he listened, and then he remembered that Griff Morgan had watched him ride out of Rimrock, alone, and Griff hated him and wanted him out of the way. Griff wouldn't know what his mission was, but if he were to find Harlan Craig and Judge Otis Brynn together on a lonely stretch of road, it might go hard with them. There were men found dead on roads like this, and the work attributed to road agents.

Riding back at a gallop to the buckboard, Harlan called sharply, "Riders up ahead. Pull off the road, Judge."

There were no trees here, but the land was broken up with huge boulders, some of them higher than a man on horseback.

Harlan pointed toward a rock which was as big as a good-sized house, and Judge Brynn immediately turned the buckboard off the road, the vehicle bumping over rocks and uneven ground.

Dismounting, Harlan, holding his own chestnut, went up ahead to lead the buckboard team around the big rock where it was completely hidden from the road.

Judge Brynn came down from the buckboard seat, and said quietly, "Are you armed, Mr. Craig?"

"I have a gun," Harlan replied.

"Were I wiser," Brynn murmured, "I would have one, also. I expected to come back earlier."

"Hold the horses," Harlan told him. "They'll probably keep on going into Windham, looking for me."

"For you?" Brynn asked him curiously.

"Griff Morgan saw me ride out of town tonight," Harlan explained. "We had it out in the street this afternoon, and I broke his nose. I believe this is his bunch coming at us."

"Morgan won't have any use for me, either." Brynn laughed softly. "He knows I'm not a United Copper man. William Andrews might give him a good-sized bonus to get me out of the way."

The little judge was very cool, and Harlan had respect for him. He watched the riders sweeping down the grade from Rimrock, and he counted eight of them. The man in the lead had a patch of white across his nose.

They hammered on, disappearing out of sight, and when they were gone, Harlan said, "We'll have to move fast. They may be coming back when they don't find me."

He led the team back to the road, and Judge Brynn picked up the reins.

"I'll cover you in the rear," Harlan said. "Keep the horses going, and turn down that back road."

"Don't get yourself in trouble on account of me," Brynn advised. "They came after you anyway. Morgan

100

mightn't have the nerve to shoot me down in cold blood. I have friends and some influence in this town. You're a new man, and no one cares too much whether you're alive or dead."

"They won't shoot either one of us down," Harlan smiled, "if we move fast enough."

Brynn got the buckboard going, and Harlan followed him at a distance of a hundred yards, both moving at a brisk pace. When they reached the crossroads, Brynn turned the buckboard off to the left, waving a hand to Harlan.

Harlan was about to follow him when he heard a shout from behind, and when he turned he saw riders bearing down on him. They were still more than a hundred yards away when one of them opened up with a gun.

Quickly, Harlan slid his own Smith & Wesson from the holster, fired twice, and then moved slowly after the retreating Judge Brynn. Brynn had whipped up the horses at the sound of the shot, and the riders who were following cut across to incercept him.

Harlan slid in between them, firing twice again, and saw one man lurch forward in the saddle and then grasp for the horn. The others slowed down, falling in behind them as they headed for Rimrock. The town was about a mile away over this smaller side road, and Harlan was quite sure he could keep the riders off for that short distance.

Several times Judge Brynn turned to look back at him, but Harlan waved him on, knowing that without a gun he was of no use.

They were swinging around the rear of the Wyandotte Mine, still about a half-mile from the town, when Harlan's horse went down. He didn't know whether the animal was hit or whether it stumbled, but very suddenly its front legs gave way, and Harlan felt himself going through the air.

Landing on his left shoulder, he rolled, his face scraping the dust of the road. The men behind him yelled triumphantly, but Harlan came up, unhurt, darting for the protection of a nearby rock.

Several bullets followed him as he flattened himself behind the rock and opened fire on the advancing riders. They split, several of them riding around, but already it was too late to intercept Judge Brynn, who was driving the buckboard down a grade and into town.

Harlan was positive Griff Morgan and his riders had come out to get him, and now that he was downed they would redouble their efforts. He saw two of them dismount and come forward, crawling.

Reloading the Smith & Wesson, he waited, firing when he saw a head coming around a bush. His chief concern was the rear, where he was unprotected. The two riders who'd gone after Judge Brynn had left him, and were returning.

They also dismounted and started to creep up on him, taking cover behind rocks and bushes. He was in a tight spot now, and he knew it. He heard Griff Morgan yell:

"Swing out — swing out."

His position here was untenable with Morgan's men encircling him, opening fire on all sides. Judge Brynn undoubtedly would send him aid, but that would take a little time. And one well-placed bullet could kill him in a second.

CHAPTER
TEN

Morgan's men were all dismounted now, and Harlan couldn't see any of them as they crawled toward him. Every once in a while a gun flashed, and he fired back, but the shadows were very deceiving, and he didn't think he'd hit anyone.

The shaft house of the Wyandotte Mine was about seventy-five yards away, and apparently deserted at this hour. A narrow road led up to it. Harlan studied the road, and the shafthouse, and then decided to take his chances. A running man did not make a good target in this dim light, and there was the possibility he would make it to the house without getting hit. If he stayed where he was, sooner or later a bullet would reach him.

Firing twice, he leaped to his feet and started up the road at top speed. Griff Morgan yelled:

"Knock him down! Knock him down!"

He kept going, with the bullets coming behind him. One slug kicked up dust very close to his right foot, but he kept going at top speed, plunging in through the half-opened doorway, and dropping to the floor just as several bullets tore through the wood.

104

Gun in hand, he crawled around the shaft and the cage, and seated himself against the wall on the far side, his gun resting on his knee and facing the door.

They had to come in at him now if they expected to get him, and they'd have to come through that door one at a time. As they came through they would be silhouetted in the doorway. He didn't think they'd be too anxious to come.

He could hear them outside. They fired several bullets in through the doorway, but he was sitting to one side and low on the floor, and none of the bullets came near him.

He waited, hearing them talking outside as they circled the building, trying to figure out a way to get in. After a while he heard distant hoofbeats, and then Morgan's men broke for their horses, and he heard them hammering away.

As he was walking down the road from the shaft he saw the riders spurring up hard. There were six of them, with Cole McAfee in the lead, and he was pleased to notice that Boyd Garrison was with them. He'd wondered whether Garrison would come.

"You all right, Harlan?" Garrison asked anxiously.

"Not a scratch," Harlan told him. "My horse went down. I fell clear, and then hid out in the Wyandotte shafthouse."

"You figured it was Griff Morgan," McAfee scowled. "Can you prove it, Craig?"

Harlan shrugged. "I saw him," he said. "No one else saw him. Reckon you'll find him in a saloon in Rimrock now, and he'll have a dozen men to prove he never even left the saloon this night." He looked at Garrison then, and asked, "Judge Brynn all right?"

"He came in through the side streets," Garrison nodded, "and then notified me that they had you down. I got McAfee, and we picked up a few boys and came out as fast as we could."

"A rotten business," McAfee said tersely. "When they try to ride a man down and kill him, I don't like it."

"I don't like it, either," Harlan told him. "He'll have to pay for it."

"What are you going to do?" Garrison wanted to know.

"We'll see," Harlan murmured, "tonight. When a man fights me in the open, I don't mind it. When he brings his dogs after me it's another story."

Cole McAfee just shook his head in disgust. "Hop up behind me," he said to Harlan. "We'll head back for town."

Back at the hotel they found Judge Brynn and Julia waiting for them inside the lobby. The streets of Rimrock were still overflowing with drunken miners who threatened to become worse as the night wore on.

Otis Brynn's pale blue eyes lighted up when he saw Harlan come in through the door.

"You all right, my boy?" he asked, shaking Harlan's hand warmly.

"I'm still alive," Harlan told him.

Julia came over also, and there was a warm glow on her face. "We are grateful to you, Mr. Craig," she said. "Father told me all about it."

Harlan noticed that Boyd Garrison was watching him closely as Julia spoke to him, but he could make nothing from Garrison's face.

"They were after me," Harlan explained. "I don't know whether they'd have caused any trouble to your father."

Boyd Garrison said jokingly, "Harlan is a very unpopular man in this town, Julia."

"Only because he works for you," Julia reminded him, "and after what has been happening I don't think I would recommend the job."

"It pays well," Harlan smiled. "I'm not doing it for love."

"No one works for the love of me," Garrison said wryly.

For one moment Harlan sympathized with the man, but then he remembered that Boyd Garrison had made his own choice. In his striving for great wealth he'd stepped hard on many people, and he'd made enemies. He was cold and ruthless and scheming where money was concerned, and men paid him back as he dealt with them.

"You're sure it was Griff Morgan after you?" Garrison asked.

"I saw his nose with the patch on it," Harlan told him. "Of course there could be other men in this town with bandages on their noses, and interested in killing me, but I doubt it."

"That's the second attempt on your life," Garrison mused. "I don't want to see you killed, Harlan. I'm almost tempted to let you go."

Harlan looked at him. "I accepted the job." He shrugged.

"What do you intend to do?" Garrison asked him.

"See Griff Morgan for one thing," Harlan told him.

Garrison grimaced. "You going to kill him?"

"I don't know," Harlan said.

"I wish you'd stay away from him," Julia Brynn murmured.

"He'll be after me," Harlan pointed out. "He'll never stop coming after me."

"Can't the law stop him?" Julia wanted to know.

Cole McAfee, who was in the lobby, said glumly, "I can't stop what's going on outside. I can't watch everybody in this town. Men who started this should stop it."

He glanced at Boyd Garrison significantly.

"My business," Garrison told him blandly, "is mining copper ore."

"Reckon you can make things tough for me," McAfee scowled, "but I can't do anything about you, can I?"

Fred Barnhouse came into the hotel, looking at everyone, his glance lingering for a moment on Julia Brynn.

"Plenty of excitement around here," he said. "What's this about somebody having you holed up at Wyandotte Mine, Harlan?"

Harlan shrugged. "I think it was Morgan and some of his crew. I can't prove it. That's the end of it as far as you're concerned, Barnhouse. You print that, and Morgan can sue you for libel."

108

"I won't print it," Barnhouse told him. "What's the story about Judge Brynn?"

Garrison explained briefly, and when he'd finished Fred Barnhouse said enviously:

"You were quite the hero, Harlan."

"Just looking after my life," Harlan said.

Judge Brynn and Julia went up to their rooms, and Harlan moved out to the porch with Garrison, Barnhouse, and Cole McAfee. Another fight had just started down in front of the Roseland Dance Hall, and McAfee headed that way, grumbling to himself and yelling for his deputies, who were stationed all along the street.

"If it were one fight," Garrison said, "he wouldn't worry about it. McAfee's concerned that it'll turn into something big."

"Are you concerned about it?" Barnhouse asked him.

"Let dog eat dog," Garrison retorted.

"Those are your men out there," Barnhouse told him. "They work for you in your mines."

"They work for wages," Garrison retorted. "If William Andrews paid them more than I, they'd leave me tomorrow, and you know it."

Harlan started down the steps to the street, and Garrison called after him, "Where are you going, Harlan?"

"Down the street," Harlan told him.

"You forget that you're working for me?"

"Fire me," Harlan challenged.

Garrison didn't say anything, and Harlan walked on, taking his time, picking his way through the crowd on the walks. A drunk lurched into him and bounced off. He swore indignantly, acted as if he would like to make something out of it, had one look at Harlan's face, and then decided to move on.

Harlan passed four saloons, pausing each time to look in over the bat-wing doors. When he glanced back once he saw Garrison standing on the porch watching him.

He found Griff Morgan in the Cheyenne Saloon, standing at the bar with several other men, drinking. Griff's clothes were dusty from riding, and the white bandage on his nose was dirty.

Shouldering his way to the bar, Harlan came up next to him. Griff had been watching him in the bar mirror, and he turned casually, that same insolent grin on his broad face, which was still swollen and cut from the fight early that afternoon.

"What can I do for you, Craig?" Griff asked.

"Doing any riding lately, Griff?" Harlan asked him.

"When?" Griff asked. "Tonight?"

"Tonight," Harlan said.

"Been here all night," Griff smiled. "Ask Charlie, the bartender."

"Asking you," Harlan said.

"You got the wrong man," Griff told him.

"I think I got the right man," Harlan stated blandly. "Some dog chased me out of Rimrock tonight, and he had his pack with him. I winged one of them, but it wasn't you."

110

"You're crazy," Griff said cheerfully.

"Am I?" Harlan asked, and he picked up a half-empty beer glass in front of him and threw the contents into Griff Morgan's face.

A man yelled nearby, and bolted for the door. Other men along the bar scrambled over each other to get out of the way of any flying bullets.

Griff backed away, spluttering, beer dripping from his chin. He wore a gun on his right hip, but he made no attempt to draw it. For several moments he couldn't see with the beer in his eyes, and Harlan watched him, his coat open and his own gun revealed, waiting for Griff to make a move.

He wasn't sure at first what Griff would do, but when the mine superintendent hesitated he was lost. Griff had time to think about dying, and that took the fight out of him. He'd been whipped physically this afternoon, and that had taken a lot of the confidence out of him. Now he was being stood up with a gun, and he knew it, and he didn't like it.

His right hand rested near the butt of the gun in his holster, but he didn't draw the gun. His fingers twitched, but they went no closer to the butt of the gun.

"Draw your gun," Harlan told him.

Griff Morgan looked at him, and his eyes seemed to be different. He was no longer the tough Griff Morgan who'd hammered men into submission with his fists and cowed them with his gun. From now on he still would be dangerous, but never from the front.

"You're pushing me too hard," Morgan rasped.

"Draw your gun," Harlan repeated, "or get out."

Griff wiped the beer from his face. His pale green eyes flitted around the room once, at the silent men watching along the walls and crowded in the doorway. Three bartenders behind the bar of the Cheyenne Saloon stood tense, ready to duck if the guns went off.

Griff Morgan's mouth twitched. He wiped more beer from his face with the back of his hand. He mumbled something under his breath, but he didn't draw his gun, and after a while Harlan heard a deep sigh run through the crowd, which was watching tensely. They, too, knew that it was over.

Quite suddenly, Griff turned and walked out of the saloon. He walked past Fred Barnhouse, who was standing to one side of the doorway, and Barnhouse looked at Harlan and shook his head lightly.

The newspaper man walked back to the hotel with Harlan, and he said as they passed through the crowd:

"You won that one. Does it make you feel any better?"

"Any man comes after me with a gun," Harlan stated, "and brings his dirty crew with him, must learn that the next time I'll shoot him."

"He'll shoot you in the back now," Barnhouse said. "Will that make you die any easier?"

"I'll watch him," Harlan replied.

They went back to the hotel, and he went up to his room, more tired and worn than he'd thought he was.

CHAPTER
ELEVEN

In the morning when Harlan came down for breakfast he found Cole McAfee camped in the dining room, hunched over a cup of coffee, a cigar in one hand, and a scowl on his face.

"You never smile," Harlan told him.

"Give me something to smile about," McAfee growled. "Biggest mines in town still closed, and won't be opened till nobody knows when. Soon as Judge Brynn opens the High Dollar, William Andrews will slap another injunction on it for some reason or other. This town's having the biggest hangover it ever knew, and nobody's feeling too good about it."

Harlan had his breakfast, and then walked down to the office of the High Dollar Mine, finding it a beehive of activity. The office was on the second floor above a dry-goods store, and Harlan found at least twenty-five persons there — clerks, lawyers, surveyors, mining engineers — all of them running in and out of Garrison's office in the rear.

Sitting down on a bench, Harlan smoked through a cigar before Garrison striding out of his office to consult with one of his engineers and spotted him. He came over immediately, and said, "Might be a little excitement up on the hill this afternoon, Harlan. We're moving lumber and equipment up there now, and we intend to start work on the new claim within a matter of hours."

"McAfee says there'll be trouble," Harlan told him.

"McAfee's job," Boyd Garrison said quietly, "is to uphold the law, and I'm within the law by mining this claim."

Harlan shrugged. "You want me around now?" he asked.

"Your time is your own," Garrison smiled, "unless I call for you." He paused. "I heard you stood up Griff Morgan last night."

"Had to do that," Harlan told him.

Garrison nodded. "I understand," he said. "Just watch him from now on."

Harlan left the office, got a horse, and rode up the hill past the closed shafthouse of the High Dollar Mine, and up to the patch of ground upon which Boyd Garrison had set his claim stakes.

The spot was a whirlwind of activity. Wagons loaded with lumber were toiling up the grade; windlasses and other mining machinery followed. Hundreds of idle miners from town had wandered up the hill to watch and to speculate.

Fred Barnhouse was there, and when he saw Harlan he came over. Harlan dismounted and stood beside the horse, watching the workmen.

"You think he'll get away with it?" Barnhouse asked sardonically.

Harlan shrugged. "Reckon I wouldn't make a guess," he said.

"You know who got off the train this morning?" Barnhouse asked him next.

Harlan shook his head.

"You've heard of the Lester brothers, John and Trev?"

Harlan frowned. "I've heard of them," he said briefly.

The Lester brothers were well-known in many Western states, and while Harlan had never run across them, he'd heard many stories concerning their skill with six-guns. Both were hired killers; both walked a precarious path along the edge of the law.

"John and Trev Lester arrived in Rimrock this morning," Fred Barnhouse said, "and I don't imagine they came to see the sights, or even to mine copper ore."

"William Andrews hired them," Harlan said.

"He's lost his big stick in Griff Morgan," Barnhouse observed, "and now he needs somebody else. There'll be plenty more coming in, which means that Garrison will have to bring in his crew, also."

Harlan nodded. It had been evident from the start that this was the way it would end.

"I understand Mr. Andrews is trying to get a court order to stop Garrison from mining on this patch."

"On what grounds?" Harlan asked curiously.

"His lawyers can find plenty of grounds," Barnhouse laughed, "or they can make some up. They can ask for a delay until a re-survey is made and they are sure Garrison is not encroaching on some of their territory."

Harlan watched the workmen as they cleared the ground and started to dig. Other groups of workmen set up windlasses under the direction of Ed Nicholson, who was in charge of operations.

The work was progressing smoothly with no outside interference as yet. The crowd watching the proceedings was in a good mood, most of them Garrison men who were behind him in his fight against United Copper. They looked upon this as a clever coup on Garrison's part.

After watching for about an hour Harlan rode back to town, Barnhouse having left earlier. He went down the main street, heading for the Empire Hotel, and as he passed the Grant, where he'd originally stayed, he saw two men sitting on the porch, rocking gently. They were not particularly impressive men, of medium height, slender in the shoulders with narrow faces, and reddish-brown hair. One man wore a mustache, and the other was clean-shaven. Except for the mustache they could have been mistaken for twins.

Harlan had never seen them before, but he was willing to stake a large bet that these men were the infamous Lester brothers. There was a coolness and a coldness about them which other men did not possess. They sat on the porch completely at ease, confident, almost insolent in their manner, both with cigars in their mouths.

As Harlan rode by they studied him leisurely and continued to rock. He wondered how Mr. Andrews intended to use these men, and others he was undoubtedly bringing into Rimrock.

116

He passed Marcia Reynolds' dress shop, and caught a glimpse of her inside, and then he rode on to the Empire Hotel to stable the horse. On coming out of the stable, instead of entering the hotel dining room to eat, he walked on down to the dress shop and opened the door.

A bell tinkled inside, and Marcia, who had been in the rear room, came out, a quick smile coming to her face when she saw him.

"Time for dinner," Harlan said. "Thought I could take you out if you didn't have any other plans."

"I don't have any other plans," Marcia laughed, "and I'd be glad to go, Harlan."

Ten minutes later they were sitting at a table in the Empire dining room when Boyd Garrison came in. Garrison strode through the door, buoyant, alive, his hat in his hand. On spotting Harlan and Marcia, his eyes lighted up, and he came over immediately.

"May I join you?" he asked. "I do hate to eat alone."

Marcia glanced at Harlan, and Harlan said resignedly, "Our pleasure."

Garrison pulled up a chair, ordered his meal, and then sat back.

"This is a great day," he said with satisfaction. "We have just begun work on the biggest ore-producing mine on the hill."

"Congratulations," Miss Reynolds told him. "I wish you success, Mr. Garrison."

"Thank you." Garrison smiled at her.

"Any trouble yet?" Harlan asked him.

"You anticipate any?" Garrison countered.

"Barnhouse just told me the two Lester brothers arrived in town, and I believe I saw them on the porch of the Grant Hotel. They're professional gun-hands."

Garrison shrugged. "Possibly just passing through."

"And possibly hired by Mr. Andrews," Harlan observed. "I'd hate to have them on my tail."

"I don't imagine they'll bother us," Garrison replied. "We'll worry about it when it happens, Harlan."

Harlan didn't say anything to that. He noticed how Garrison turned his attention to Marcia Reynolds, commanding all of her attention even though she was supposedly dining with Harlan.

He was interested in her dress shop, and in her plans, and he asked questions. He was the kind, courteous, helpful friend, not the mining wizard of the West.

When they finished eating, Garrison excused himself and hurried back to his office. Harlan walked Marcia back to the dress shop, and again he saw the two Lester brothers on the porch of the Grant Hotel. This time Griff Morgan was with them, sitting on the porch rail, his back toward the street.

Griff turned to look over at him as he went past, and Harlan noticed that he had a fresh bandage across his broken nose.

"I am obliged for the dinner," Marcia said. "It was kind of you."

"My pleasure," Harlan told her. "We'll have to do it again."

That afternoon he found time hanging heavy on his hands.

118

He walked up the grade to watch the work on Garrison's new mine which was already christened the Big Bonanza. The shafthouse was almost up, and some of the machinery in place. Big, red-headed Ed Nicholson was directing the work, sweating, shouting at the men, very efficient at his job.

By nightfall Harlan had decided that Garrison's money was not sufficient to recompense him for this life of boredom, and had made up his mind to resign. He had an idea where he could get another job in this town without too much effort.

Garrison's office was still a beehive of activity at seven in the evening when Harlan went up the stairs. Garrison was having a conference with several of his engineers, and it was another half-hour before he'd finished and was ready to leave. He came over, slipped an expensive cigar in Harlan's coat pocket, and said:

"It's been a big day, Harlan. Everything going according to schedule."

"That right?" Harlan murmured.

"Anything on your mind?" Garrison asked him. "I told you you didn't have to wait around."

"Wanted to see you," Harlan said. "I'm resigning."

Garrison looked at him curiously. "Getting too tough?" he asked.

Harlan smiled faintly. "Reckon I don't like the work," he said.

Garrison frowned. "I don't like to lose you, Harlan," he said. "You're good for me; you're an honest man." Harlan could see he was honestly disappointed.

"You should have more honest men around you," Harlan told him, "but I'm through."

"What are you going to do?"

"Look for other work."

"I'll give you other work," Garrison told him. "I'll give you any kind of job you want. You can work along with Ed Nicholson. He'll teach you the ropes."

Harlan hesitated for one moment, and then he shook his head. Working for Boyd Garrison on any kind of job would amount to the same thing. He'd be paid well, but gradually Garrison would begin to own him the way he owned other men. He'd become dependent upon the money, and upon his position.

"You don't want it?" Garrison asked, disappointed.

"No," Harlan said.

"You can draw your pay at the desk," Garrison muttered, and nodded toward a clerk at one of the desks.

After pocketing the few dollars which were due him, Harlan went down to the street, turning left. He walked one block through the crowds, noticing that they were as noisy and as riotous as on the previous night.

When he reached Cole McAfee's office, and the town jail, he turned in. The building was of brick, but very small, wedged in between two larger frame structures. One of McAfee's deputies, a big, red-faced man, was hauling in a drunk as Harlan approached, and the drunk was whooping at the top of his voice, trying to break away.

Harlan followed the deputy and the drunk into the tiny office, and grinned at the expression of disgust on McAfee's face.

"Where we gonna put 'em, Dave?" McAfee asked. "We got sixteen in here now, and this jail holds eight."

"Want me to take him back?" Dave grinned. "He was gettin' real loud in the Montana Saloon, tellin' everybody he was gonna shoot up Boyd Garrison. Had a gun on him, too, but I don't think he's got the nerve to use it."

"Put me outa work," the drunk yelled. "Me with seven kids."

"And you're blowing your money in the Montana Saloon," McAfee snapped. "You use a gun on Garrison and we'll hang you higher than a kite."

The drunk gulped, and sobered a little. "He ain't got no right puttin' a man outa work," he growled.

"His mine, his money," McAfee told him. "Nobody's making you live in this town, mister." To the deputy he said, "Let him go, Dave, but don't give him his gun. If he makes any more trouble we'll put him down in the hole in the cellar."

Dave pushed the drunk out into the street, and Cole McAfee turned to Harlan, who was waiting near the door, smiling.

"It's not so funny," McAfee growled. "This goes on all night, and it'll go on till those two big mines are opened and the men are working again. It'll get worse every night, too, because they'll be getting ugly after a while."

Harlan nodded sympathetically. "You have a tough job," he said.

Cole McAfee looked at him. "And you have a tougher one," he said slowly. "You've heard the Lester boys are in Rimrock?"

Harlan nodded. "Saw them."

"Your job is to keep Boyd Garrison alive," McAfee observed. "It might get a little tough now."

"I just quit," Harlan told him.

McAfee glanced at him quickly. "Not because of the Lesters," he said. "I know that much."

"Not because of the Lesters." Harlan smiled. "I don't like following a man around like a dog."

"Figured that would gall you after a while." McAfee grinned. "You're not built for that kind of work. What happens now?"

Harlan sat down in a battered chair and tilted it against the wall. He looked at the fly-specked posters on the bulletin board behind McAfee's roll-top desk, and he said:

"How many deputies you run in this town, McAfee?"

"Three," McAfee told him glumly. "I could use thirty the way this town's going."

"What do you pay?" Harlan asked.

"Hundred a month and keep," McAfee said. "It's not a fortune. We stay at a boarding house down the street."

"Now you have four deputies if you want another one," Harlan said. "You want to pin a star on me?"

Cole McAfee looked at him, and then he reached back to the desk and picked up a metal, five-pointed star, tossing it into Harlan's lap.

122

"You're on," he said. "Reckon you know what you're getting into with the Lesters here, and maybe another couple of dozen gunmen coming off the trains within the next week or so, and three thousand idle men roaming the streets."

"I know what I'm getting into," Harlan agreed, and pinned the star on his vest.

"You'll want to move out of Garrison's place," McAfee said. "We're in Mrs. Miller's, next to the Silver Dollar Saloon." He leaned forward, held out his hand and said quietly, "Luck. Let's hope both of us live to a decent age, but I doubt it."

CHAPTER
TWELVE

Harlan went back to the Empire House, up the stairs, and opened the door of his room to find the Lester brothers sitting there, both with cigars in their mouths, their hats on the back of their heads.

Neither of them got up as he closed the door behind him. He noticed that the door leading to Garrison's suite was closed, too, and he didn't hear any sounds in the other rooms. Garrison was probably out at this time having his evening meal.

One brother had a golden-brown mustache, and he spoke in soft, modulated tones. He said, "Waitin' for you, Craig."

Harlan looked at him, and then walked over to the bed and stooped down to bring out his suitcase. He started to pack it, while both brothers watched him silently.

"You're a wise man," the mustached Lester said.

"Am I?" Harlan murmured without even looking at him.

"You know who we are?"

"I don't give a hoot," Harlan said. "You're in my room, and I ought to throw you both out, but I'm leaving anyway."

"You'd have a time throwin' us out," the other. Lester said. "I'm Trev Lester, and this is my brother, John."

They both had soupy green eyes, very unpleasant eyes, and narrow chins. Their shoulders sloped, which made their necks seem longer than they were. Both men wore dark clothes. Trev Lester's coat was open, and Harlan could see the Colt .44 in the holster underneath.

"We came here," John Lester said casually, "to tell you to get out of town, Craig. Reckon we came a little late."

"Tell me now," Harlan said, straightening up. His coat was pulled back, revealing the star.

Both men saw the badge, and Trev Lester scratched his chin thoughtfully.

"You change jobs fast, mister," he said. "Now you're a lawman."

"Any time you want to see me," Harlan said, "you'll find me around."

"That right?" Trev Lester said thoughtfully.

They were not twins, and he seemed to be the younger man, although not by much. Harlan figured them to be in their early thirties.

"You wear a tin badge," John Lester said, "and you get tough. That how it goes, Craig?"

"I was tough before I wore the badge," Harlan told him. "Ask Griff Morgan."

"You don't fight us with your fists." John Lester smiled. "You know that. When you come you come with a gun, and make sure it's loaded."

"It'll be loaded," Harlan promised him. "What is it you want me to do now?"

The older Lester was a little perplexed. "Heard you were Garrison's bodyguard, and you worked over a man named Griff Morgan," he said. "We aimed to send you out of town. Now you don't work for Garrison. That it?"

"That's it." Harlan nodded, closed the suitcase and picked it up. "You boys came in here to tell me something. Now I'll tell you something. I quit Garrison because I didn't like the work, and now I'm a deputy sheriff in this town. I'm hired to uphold the law. You cross it, and you'll have to answer to me."

"Reckon you're real tough," Trev Lester drawled.

"Stay around," Harlan advised, "and you'll find out."

"We're stayin'," Trev told him, "an you'll be findin' out."

Harlan left them sitting there and went down the stairs. At the bottom of the steps he met Julia Brynn coming up; she glanced at the suitcase in his hand.

"You're not leaving?" she said quickly.

Harlan pulled back his coat to reveal the star. "I signed up with Cole McAfee," he said. "I'm leaving Garrison."

"You didn't have any disagreement?"

Harlan smiled. "Got tired of the job," he told her. "It's not what I wanted."

"I suppose Mr. McAfee needs more deputies," Julia said. "Father thinks the town will be getting worse until the companies are back in operation."

"It's rough now," Harlan admitted. "McAfee has his jailhouse filled all the time."

Behind him he heard the two Lester brothers coming down the stairs, and he stepped aside to let them pass.

Julia glanced after them, and said, "They're new in town, aren't they, Harlan?"

"They're new," Harlan admitted. He gave her no further information.

"I'm glad you're staying in Rimrock at any rate," she said, and some color came to her face. "I have been deeply grateful to you for going out after my father last night."

Harlan watched the two Lesters going out through the front door of the hotel, and said thoughtfully, "I'd advise your father to stay in town from now on until this trouble blows over."

"You think there could be trouble for him?"

Harlan shrugged. "I wouldn't take too many chances," he said. "There's always one faction won't like a judge's decisions."

"Father is stubborn," Julia murmured. "If I told him to remain in town he'd deliberately go out." She added, "He's out now, by the way."

"Where?" Harlan asked.

"On Tuesdays he goes up to Saddletop to hold court. He stays over for the night and returns in the morning."

"Where is Saddletop?" Harlan wanted to know.

"Five miles north," Julia explained. "It's another small mining town, and it's in Father's district. He goes up in his buckboard."

"When he gets back," Harlan said, "you'd better tell him what I said."

"He still won't listen," Julia smiled, "but I'll tell him."

She went on up to her room, and Harlan walked down the street to register and deposit his suitcase in the room at Mrs. Miller's boarding house. He spent the remainer of the evening till past two o'clock in the morning working with McAfee and the other deputies; the work consisted mainly of stopping fights which threatened to get out of hand, and hauling recalcitrant drunks to the jailhouse.

McAfee released those who were beginning to sober up, making room for the others as they came in.

Several times Harlan saw the two Lesters, once in the Cheyenne Saloon playing cards, and another time at the bar of the Montana Saloon. They watched him handle a big miner, subduing the man with a stiff blow to the stomach when he tried to fight. They watched with their expressionless faces, and their dull green eyes, and they puffed on their cigars.

At two-thirty in the morning McAfee said, "Take a break, boys, and forget the rest of 'em. If they want to take each other apart, let 'em do it. I'll stick on with Dave till morning. Rest of you are off duty till noon tomorrow."

As the men were leaving he said to Harlan, "How did it go?"

Harlan looked at his bruised knuckles ruefully. He'd been in a fight with two Bengal Tiger miners, both of whom had been only partly drunk, and very ugly, and he'd managed to subdue them with the help of Dave Bannion, the other deputy, but it had been a fight.

"It's better than tailing after Boyd Garrison," Harlan said.

"Thought you'd like it," McAfee responded. "It's honest work, and you earn your dollar. Let Garrison look after himself if he wants to turn this town upside down to make a million."

Harlan hadn't seen Garrison all evening, nor had he run across Griff Morgan, which was unusual. He wondered if Griff had decided to leave Rimrock after being publicly disgraced. He didn't think Griff would run until he'd settled his little score.

"Get some sleep," McAfee was saying. "You'll need it."

Harlan went back to the boarding house, dead tired, but not so tired that he didn't hear the explosion some time later. It was a dynamite explosion somewhere up on the hill, and he assumed a night crew was working at one of the mines. In the morning, at breakfast in Mrs. Miller's kitchen, Dave Bannion informed him that a crew of men had chased Garrison's guards away from the new Big Bonanza Mine, and dynamited the partially completed shafthouse.

"Andrews' crew," Bannion said wearily. "McAfee an' me went up there on the run, but it was all over when we arrived. Garrison will have to start over again. Reckon he didn't figure Mr. Andrews would let him get away with it."

"Now it'll be a real fight," Harlan scowled. "An out and out fight with no holds barred."

"McAfee says a lot more hardcases got off the trains this morning. Reckon we have our work cut out for us, Harlan."

"The big ones are the Lesters," Harlan mused. "We take them down and the others will walk easy. They have the reputations."

"Who's taking them down?" Bannion asked dubiously. "Not a man in town can match their guns."

"They can't walk around like they owned the town," Harlan told him. "When they cross the line they'll have to be stopped."

Bannion grinned. "I'm for it."

Harlan walked down to the marshal's office after eating, had a look at the drunks sprawled on the floors of the cells, and came out to the front of the building. It was nearly eleven o'clock in the morning by now, as he'd gotten up late after his long stint the night before. Cole McAfee had returned to the boarding house at dawn and was sleeping.

The morning was bright and fairly clear, a west wind having blown away some of the sulphur fumes from the smelters. Harlan stepped out into the sunshine on the walk, and saw Julia Brynn coming toward the office.

Even before she'd reached him he knew that she was in trouble. It was in her face, in her eyes.

Harlan touched his hat when she came up. "You looking for the law, Miss Brynn?"

"I'm worried about Father," she told him. "He usually returns early in the morning if he stays over. His buckboard hasn't come in."

Harlan frowned. "He may have decided to spend another day in Saddletop."

"He'd have sent word," Julia said worriedly. "After what you said yesterday, I'm afraid something may have happened."

"I'll ride up," Harlan volunteered. "I might meet him on the way in."

"It's kind of you," Julia told him.

Cole McAfee had several saddle horses in a shed at the rear of the jailhouse. Cole threw a saddle on a black gelding and rode out of town, taking the wagon road north.

He passed a string of ore wagons coming down from one of the mines, heading for the smelters on the other side of town. One of the drivers yelled at him and waved a hand, recognizing him as the man who'd whipped Griff Morgan.

Harlan nodded back and kept riding. A mile or so out of town the atmosphere cleared. Brown buffalo grass covered the hills, which around Rimrock were barren of vegetation. A tiny stream dissected the hills, and cottonwoods and willows grew along the fringe of the stream. It was pretty country beyond the mining area.

To the north he saw the smoke from the lone smelter at Saddletop, and occasionally he caught glimpses of the road as it twisted through the hills.

He didn't see Judge Brynn's buckboard until he was more than halfway to Saddletop, and then the buckboard wasn't on the road. A hundred yards or more down a side path which led to the stream which paralleled the road at this point, he saw the buckboard and the team half-hidden among the willows. Wheel tracks led down toward the creek, although he couldn't imagine why the Judge had turned off here, unless it was to water the horses.

As he turned down the side path he didn't see Judge Brynn up on the seat of the buckboard, and his worries increased. Dismounting, he walked forward, and one of the horses, a dapple gray, whinnied at him. This seemed to be a regular watering place for horses along the road from Saddlerock, but the horses had drunk their fill and wanted to move again.

The seat was empty, but Harlan found Judge Brynn on the ground on the left side of the wagon, half-hidden among the bushes where he'd fallen.

Running forward, he knelt and rolled the man over, seeing the blood on his white shirt front. Judge Brynn's blue eyes fluttered open as Harlan moved him, and he said weakly:

"Who is it?"

He was gone. Harlan could tell from the color of his face. The blood was draining from his body, and it was only a miracle that he was still alive. Even his lips had turned grayish, and a trickle of blood came from his mouth.

"I'm Harlan Craig," Harlan told him. "Can I do anything for you?"

"A little water." The Judge managed to smile. "Can't get to it. So close, but I can't get to it."

Harlan found a pail in the wagon, ran down to the stream to scoop some water up, and then hurried back.

He thought the Judge had already died when he came back, but again Brynn opened his small, pale blue eyes.

Harlan managed to trickle some of the water into his mouth.

"You know who shot you, Judge Brynn?" he asked.

Otis Brynn swallowed the water, closed his eyes, then opened them again. He said quite calmly, "Griff Morgan. I saw the bandage across his face after I'd fallen from the seat. He was up on the grade to the east of the road, shooting down from a crevice."

"How'd you get down here?" Harlan asked him.

"Horses run loose after the shot. I fell back on the buckboard, and then dropped to the ground when they stopped here."

"You're sure it was Morgan?" Harlan asked slowly.

"Know him," Judge Brynn murmured. "Came up closer to have a better look at me, and to make sure I was dead. I saw him."

Harlan looked around. "I'll see if I can get you to town," he said. "That bullet wound might not be so bad."

"Don't joke," Otis Brynn told him wearily. "I know when I'm finished."

He lay there, staring up at the leaves of the trees overhead, and blood again trickled from his mouth.

"You're an honest man, Craig," Brynn said softly. "Can you hear me?"

Harlan nodded. "I hear you."

"I can trust you. I can't trust too many people in Rimrock."

"All right," Harlan said.

"I don't want my Julia to marry Boyd Garrison," Judge Brynn whispered. "Do you hear that, Craig?"

Harlan grimaced. "I hear it," he said.

"He's no good for her. She has no mother, and I've been the only one to advise her. Don't let her marry him."

"Don't worry about it," Harlan told him. "We'll get you into town."

"Not me." Otis Brynn smiled. "Not me."

He died then.

Harlan watched his eyelids flutter, and the heavy breathing stopped. The Judge's head rolled to one side, and when Harlan felt for a heartbeat there was none.

Harlan straightened up. He walked back to the buckboard, found an old horse blanket, and draped it over the body of the dead man. Then he took the team out of the traces and let them graze along the bank of the stream.

Then he went back to the road, and turned north in the direction of Saddletop, riding into its main street an hour later, some time past high noon.

Saddletop was not Rimrock, the copper queen of the state. There were a few producing copper mines up in the hills, and one smelter. The single street contained a half-dozen saloons, a ramshackle hotel, and a barber shop.

Harlan pulled up in front of the first saloon and dismounted. The saloon was empty. The bartender looked at Harlan over the bat-wing doors, and then went back to reading his paper. In the second saloon on the street, adjoining the barber shop, Harlan saw two men playing cards; the bar was empty.

Griff Morgan was in the third saloon, a smaller establishment, bearing the name Lulu Belle.

When Harlan pushed in through the doors, Griff spun around quickly, setting his shot glass on the wood. Harlan nodded to him impersonally and walked to the bar, stopping about eight feet away. At eight feet a man couldn't miss with a six-gun.

The bandage on Griff's nose was dirty, and his pale green eyes bloodshot. He looked dirty, too, as if he'd been holed up in the hills for some time.

He said gruffly to Harlan, "What brings you to Saddletop, Craig?"

"You," Harlan said simply. "I'm arresting you for the murder of Judge Otis Brynn."

CHAPTER
THIRTEEN

The shock showed on Griff's face. He took a short step backward along the bar, his eyes never leaving Harlan's face.

"I'm a duly authorized deputy," Harlan said. "Sworn in yesterday by Cole McAfee. You're under arrest for the killing of Judge Brynn, Morgan. Unbuckle that gunbelt and let it drop to the floor."

"You're crazy," Griff murmured. "You're real crazy, Craig."

"Drop the gunbelt," Harlan told him, "and then walk out through that door."

The bartender was watching them from behind the bar, a small, thin-faced man with a black mustache and black eyebrows.

A fly buzzed around Griff Morgan's head, and then moved over to the bartender, and the bartender waved mechanically at it with his hand.

"You're crazy," Griff said, and he drew his gun.

Harlan shot him through the middle as his gun was coming up level with his body. Griff took a step forward, an expression of mute surprise on his face. He reached for the bar, couldn't find it, and collapsed on the floor, his hat rolling from his head.

136

Harlan had a look at him, and then he said to the bartender, "You have a coroner in this town?"

"We do," the bartender muttered.

"Call him over," Harlan said.

He turned and went out through the doors and into the sunshine. A number of men were approaching from different directions, having heard the shot. They watched him silently as he mounted and rode off, heading back toward Rimrock.

He passed Judge Brynn's buckboard, noticing that no one had been there. The horses were still grazing along the stream, and the buckboard was where he'd left it.

He rode on, liking the task ahead of him less and less. Someone had to tell Julia Brynn that her father was dead, and it wasn't going to be pleasant.

When he arrived in Rimrock it was already late afternoon, and Cole McAfee was the first man to see him. McAfee was coming out of his office when Harlan rode up, and immediately Harlan turned his horse over toward the tie rack. He didn't dismount, and he gave McAfee the news from the saddle.

"Judge Brynn!" the marshal gasped. "And he says it was Griff Morgan?"

"He saw Morgan," Harlan told him. "There was no doubt in his mind."

"We'll get up a posse," McAfee grated. "We'll bring in the dog."

"You'll have to bring in a dead man," Harlan told him quietly. "I caught up with Griff in a saloon in Saddletop. He pulled his gun on me."

Cole McAfee was still staring at him as he pulled his horse around and headed up toward the Empire Hotel. After tying the horse outside, he went into the lobby and saw Boyd Garrison talking with Ed Nicholson in one corner of the lobby. He was tempted for a moment to tell Garrison the news first, but he changed his mind, lifted a hand to Garrison in greeting, and then went on up the stairs to Judge Brynn's rooms.

Julia opened immediately upon his knock. She looked at his face, and turned pale as she stepped back to let him in.

"It's bad, isn't it?" she said slowly.

Harlan stood there with his hat in his hand. He turned it around in his hands, holding the brim, and he said:

"I'm afraid your father's dead, Julia."

She didn't collapse, and she didn't cry, and he admired her for this more than he'd admired any woman he'd ever known.

"What happened?" she asked.

Harlan told her briefly. He told her everything except her father's statement regarding Boyd Garrison.

"You killed Morgan," she said.

"I asked him to turn in his gun and come with me," Harlan stated. "He wouldn't do it. We'd have hanged him anyway."

She walked to the window and stood there with her back to him, looking out, and then she said with a tremor in her voice:

"Will you notify the coroner, Harlan?"

"I'll take care of it," Harlan told her. "Anything I can do?"

"I'm all right," she said. She still didn't turn around. "I'm obliged to you, Harlan."

He went out then, and downstairs Garrison was waiting for him, curiosity in his eyes.

"You see Julia?" he asked.

There was no jealousy in his voice; he was simply curious, knowing that Harlan did not normally make visits like this.

"Judge Brynn was shot to death this morning," Harlan told him. "I had to tell her."

Garrison stared at him, and for the first time Harlan saw some small doubt come into his brown eyes. In Garrison's deck of cards Judge Brynn had been the joker; he needed Brynn; his whole plot to defeat United Copper in Rimrock depended upon the Judge being his man, and now with Brynn dead all of his plans could go awry.

"I'm sorry to hear about that," Garrison murmured, and steered Harlan in toward the hotel bar to hear the rest of the story.

Cole McAfee joined them as Harlan gave him the details.

"Andrews sent Morgan after Judge Brynn," Harlan said quietly, "but we'll never be able to prove that."

Fred Barnhouse came in hurriedly, anxious for the news, McAfee having tipped him off.

"We can't prove it." McAfee scowled. "You can't prove anything in this town."

"The bench will be empty," Barnhouse murmured, "until a new judge is appointed, and I'm thinking Mr. Andrews will do everything in his power to keep it empty for as long as possible. Without any court orders to bother him, he'll be a hard man to stop."

"How is Julia taking it?" Garrison asked.

"She can take it," Harlan told him, and again Garrison glanced at him curiously.

"Andrews' gunsharps are going to run wild in this town," Barnhouse observed. "You boys have your work cut out for you."

"We'll see how wild they run," McAfee said grimly. He looked at Harlan. "I wouldn't be surprised if Mr. Andrews sent the Lesters after you now that you killed his top man."

Harlan nodded, and said nothing.

Boyd Garrison pushed away from the bar. He said, "I'm going up to see Julia for a minute. She'll need someone to settle her affairs."

When Garrison had gone Harlan said to Barnhouse, "What about that work on the Big Bonanza Mine? Garrison rebuilding after the trouble last night?"

"Had his crew setting up another shafthouse," Barnhouse nodded. "He'll have his own armed guard there tonight."

"Then there'll be a fight?"

Barnhouse shrugged. "I don't know till tonight comes," he said.

Harlan looked at McAfee. "Where do we fit in here?" he asked. "We supposed to stop this?"

140

"Had my way," McAfee told him grimly, "I'd let dog eat dog, but there has to be law somewhere. Figure our first move is to see Andrews himself. Now."

"You won't get much out of him," Barnhouse said.

"We'll see," McAfee growled, and he left with Harlan.

The office of United Copper was down the street, a block beyond Garrison's office. Harlan returned his horse to the stable behind the jailhouse, and then walked on with McAfee.

The streets were still crowded, and McAfee informed Harlan that earlier in the afternoon he and the deputies had broken up a fight which had threatened to turn into a wholesale riot.

"Once they get loose," McAfee said, "it'll go hard on this town. If these boys don't get back to work soon, they'll tear this town up."

"Maybe we can persuade Andrews to rescind his court order on the High Dollar," Harlan said, "and then talk Garrison into letting the Bengal Tiger open up."

"Andrews won't do that." McAfee shook his head. "He's convinced Garrison is taking copper ore out of the Bengal Tiger Mine. If the mines reopen, Garrison will go right on as he was before."

"Then we'll tell Garrison," Harlan growled.

"He'll swear he's mining his own ore," McAfee said. "I'm no mining man. For all I know, maybe he is, and maybe Andrews is in the wrong." He added, "He's legally right about this Big Bonanza claim, too. He was just smart enough to think up something like that. It's just inside the law, and we can't touch him."

They entered the office of United Copper, a considerably bigger place of business than Garrison's, occupying the ground floor of a large frame building.

A clerk with green-tinted spectacles came over and said, "What can I do for you, Marshal?"

"Mr. Andrews in?" McAfee asked him.

"I'll tell him you're here," the clerk said, and went to the inner office. He came back in a few moments. "Mr. Andrews will see you."

They found the wealthy financier in a small, beautifully furnished room at the rear of the office. He sat behind a huge mahogany desk, seeming very small and frail behind it, his thin, blue-veined hands folded in front of him, a faint, cold smile on his gray face.

"This is a pleasure," he said.

"Not for me," McAfee told him bluntly. "Came in to tell you that Judge Brynn was shot dead this morning by your man, Griff Morgan, and Griff Morgan was killed in turn by Harlan when he resisted arrest."

There was no expression on Mr. Andrews' face. His gray eyes flicked over to Harlan, and then back again.

"I regret Judge Brynn's death," he stated softly. "Will you convey my condolences to his family?"

"We figure Morgan didn't shoot Brynn down on his own," McAfee said grimly. "A man needs a reason to kill another man from ambush."

"What would you suggest was his reason?" Andrews purred.

"You have any idea?" McAfee snapped.

"You are holding yourself open for a libel suit." Mr. Andrews smiled. "Even the law cannot malign a man's character."

Cole McAfee took a deep breath. "All right," he said, "we can't pin anything on you. There's something. For the good of this town I'd like you to withdraw that court order so the High Dollar Mine can open. I'm telling Garrison the same thing. These big mines have to be opened to get the men off the streets."

"What if we both refuse?"

"There'll be trouble," McAfee told him. "There's been plenty of trouble already, but it's only the beginning. These men are getting mean now. We're trying to keep them in line, but they might get out of hand."

"We can always call in the militia." Mr. Andrews smiled. "I have never been too concerned about the public because it is not concerned about me. I will reopen the High Dollar Mine on one condition."

"What is that?" McAfee asked.

"That Boyd Garrison sell every possession he has in Rimrock to me. All of his mine holdings; his new Big Bonanza claim; everything."

Cole McAfee stared at the little man, and then looked at Harlan, and Harlan knew that this was news to him, too.

"You made an offer to Garrison?" McAfee asked.

"I'll make the offer through you," Andrews told him. "I am prepared to pay Mr. Garrison one million dollars for his holdings, on the condition that he leave this town and never return."

"A million dollars," McAfee murmured.

"On the other hand," William Andrews went on slowly, "if he wants a fight he shall have a fight. We shall fight him for every foot of land on the hill. He may prevent us from mining even one pound of copper ore, but we shall stop him, also, and I think we have more capital behind us than he has behind him. I believe my offer is generous. If he persists in fighting me, eventually I shall break him."

"We'll tell him," McAfee muttered.

"Good afternoon, gentlemen." William Andrews smiled, and his face was thin and bony and gray, the face of a corpse.

Outside, McAfee said thoughtfully, "If Garrison were gone there would be peace in this town. Of course Andrews would run the whole business, and he's no easy boss, but he won't live forever, and it might be better some day. With both Garrison and Andrews here it'll always be a fight. They don't lose anything when their mines are closed for a week or so, but these poor boys down in the mines feel it when they lose a week's pay."

"You think Garrison will do it?" Harlan asked.

McAfee shook his head. "Reckon I don't know," he confessed. "Garrison will have his pile without having to fight for it. He's smart enough to know that if he fights Andrews he may lose, and he'll end with nothing. On the other hand, maybe Garrison wants the whole hog."

144

They walked back along the street toward the hotel, and when they were passing Marcia Reynolds' shop, Harlan said:

"Want to ask Miss Reynolds to stop in and see Julia. Reckon you'll talk to Garrison alone, anyway."

"Go ahead," McAfee told him.

He walked on, and Harlan turned in at the shop. Marcia was working on a dress when he came in, but she put it down immediately, flashing him a quick smile.

"You're sober this afternoon, Harlan," she said, and then the smile left her face when he didn't respond. "Anything wrong?" she asked.

"Judge Brynn was shot to death this morning," he said quietly. "Be nice if you stopped in to see Julia Brynn."

"I'm terribly sorry," Marcia murmured. "How did it happen?"

Harlan gave her the brief details, and as he was talking she put the kettle over the stove and started to make coffee.

"You'll have a cup," she said when he'd finished. "You've had a hard day, too, Harlan."

He watched her set out two cups, and then he relaxed in the chair. It was comfortable and quiet here in the rear of the store. The noises of the street reached them faintly.

He watched her hands as she worked. They were perfectly formed, long-fingered, and yet not the hands of the idle rich. Marcia Reynolds made a living with her hands, and it was an honest living.

As Harlan watched her she said, "I'm very sorry about Julia's loss. I know how she feels. I lost my father when I was fifteen."

"She's alone," Harlan said, "as you're alone." He added, "You've always gotten by. I admire you for that."

"Do you?" she said, and she looked at him steadily.

"I've always admired you," he said, and then he reached out and took her hand.

She didn't draw it away. She stood there looking down at him, and she said, "You could go far, Harlan. You have drive and power. You could go higher than Garrison if you had a mind to, and didn't mind stepping on other people."

"I mind stepping on other people," Harlan said.

"You'll never be rich," she told him, and a wistful note crept into her voice. "You'll make out, but you'll never make out on the scale that Garrison does."

"I know that, too," he said. "Does money mean an awful lot to you, Marcia?"

"Only if you've been without it, do you realize how important it is. I've been without it, Harlan."

"I, too," he said.

"It's different with a man. A man can dig ditches."

"I can never give you what Garrison can give you," he said.

"I know that, too," she said, and she looked down at him thoughtfully.

He stood up and pulled her close and kissed her, and he felt her respond.

"I like you, Harlan," she whispered. "I like you very much, but you'll never give me what I've got to have. I must drive along the boulevards in Chicago and New York in my own carriage. I used to watch them when I was a little girl. I've got to have that, Harlan. Can you understand?"

"I understand," he said. He sat down and stirred his coffee aimlessly.

"I came here," she said quietly, "for the express purpose of meeting Mr. Garrison. Can you believe that, Harlan?"

"I believe it," he said.

"If he's in love with Julia Brynn," Marcia went on, "I'll not interfere, but if he's not, I want to be there when they call it quits. I want to be first in line."

"I think you are."

CHAPTER
FOURTEEN

Harlan was eating his supper in the lunch room, alone, when Cole McAfee came in with Dan Bannion. McAfee ordered before speaking to Harlan, and then he said glumly:

"Garrison wants a million and a half to pull out of Rimrock. He won't make the deal with Andrews for a penny less."

"Are his holdings worth that much?" Harlan asked.

McAfee shrugged. "Who can tell how much ore there is in the earth? His mines might be worth five million, and they might be worth a hundred thousand. You don't know till you dig."

"So the fight goes on," Harlan mused. "I don't suppose Mr. Andrews will go that high."

"He won't," McAfee growled. "Already saw him. Says it's a steal."

"Garrison wants protection tonight up at the Big Bonanza," Dave Bannion said.

"We have to give it to him," McAfee said grimly. "Harlan, you want to take Bannion and keep an eye on Garrison's new mine?"

Harlan nodded, and looked at Bannion.

"What happens if they try another raid?" Bannion asked.

"You're a law officer," Cole McAfee said quietly. "You're upholding the law, Dave."

"All I want to know," Bannion murmured.

Later, he rode up the hill with Harlan, and they dismounted near the new shafthouse of the Big Bonanza. Garrison had a dozen men on guard with rifles, and they stared at the two lawmen suspiciously when they rode up.

"Take it easy," Bannion said. "Don't start workin' them guns till you know what you're shootin' at."

"Anybody raids this place," one of the guards grinned, "we'll know who it is, an' he'll get a belly full o' lead, Bannion."

"Seen more than one man get a belly full of lead didn't deserve it," Bannion observed. "You boys don't do any shootin' until you hear from us."

Harlan tied his horse near the shafthouse, and then sat down on some lumber to roll a cigarette. The night was cool, with plenty of stars, but no moon.

One of the guards said, "Figured we'd start a big bonfire, Dave, so's we could see 'em when they came up."

"They'd see you quicker than you'd see them," Bannion stated. "Keep the lights out all around. When you see anybody sing out."

Harlan smoked his cigarette, and then took a walk around the partially built shafthouse. It was past nine o'clock in the evening now, still early if another raid was planned for tonight.

The night lagged, and Harlan started to wish that Cole McAfee had kept him in town. He wondered if McAfee had deliberately sent him up here tonight to avoid a showdown with the two Lesters.

At about eleven o'clock in the evening one of the guards slipped down the hill and came back with a few quarts of whiskey. Harlan and Dave Bannion didn't know about it till near midnight when they heard laughter on the other side of the shafthouse.

Bannion said grimly, "Them boys have found some bug juice, Harlan."

"Might help them to shoot straighter." Harlan scowled. "Could be Mr. Andrews' money paid for that liquor."

"Reckon we'd better be on our toes, then," Bannion told him.

Thirty minutes later they heard shots and then quick yells from the direction of the High Dollar shafthouse a little farther down the hill. Dave Bannion, who had been watching on the far side of the new shafthouse, came over to Harlan quickly.

"What's that?" he asked.

A rider, spurring up the grade hard, gave them the answer a few moments later.

"Raid on the High Dollar!" he yelled. "Must be Andrews' crew."

The shooting was still going on down below. They could see the flashes of gunfire in the night.

The crew Garrison had hired hesitated for a few moments, and then started down the grade, yelling.

"Let's get 'em." Bannion scowled. "They're hittin' at the High Dollar instead of the Big Bonanza tonight."

"We better wait," Harlan said.

Bannion stared at him in the darkness. "Wait?" he repeated. "They're raidin' Garrison's property down below."

"Maybe just to draw us off," Harlan murmured. "Reckon I'd like to make sure before I went down there."

"We'll make sure," Bannion told him. "Let's get behind this lumber."

They crouched down behind the lumber pile and waited, guns drawn. Down below they were still shooting, but it seemed to be slackening off.

Bannion said softly, "Somebody coming up, Harlan."

Harlan saw a shadow slide by around the corner of the shafthouse, and then another.

"All right," he whispered.

Both men got up and moved toward the corner of the shafthouse, around the opposite side from the one where the raiders had gone. There were only two of them. They could see the men crouching at one corner of the building, and Bannion whispered:

"Settin' up a dynamite charge."

Harlan lifted his gun. He said softly, "That's it, boys. Stand up, and don't go for your guns."

He didn't know whether they were going to obey him or not, but he was ready, the gun steady in his hand. Bannion stood a little to one side, his gun also lined on the two men.

Harlan watched them stand up. He couldn't see their faces in the darkness. He could only see that one man was taller than the other.

"We ain't got guns, mister," one of them said. "Just come up here to look around."

"For what?" Bannion snapped.

"Turn around," Harlan ordered, "and start walking down the hill."

They obeyed him, drawing away from the shaft-house, but he still couldn't tell if they were armed. It seemed unlikely that two men coming up on an expedition like this would come without guns.

He wanted to get them away from the dynamite charges, however, and when they were a dozen feet from the building he ordered them to stop. They were quite close together, and very possibly they had been whispering. He called sharply to Bannion:

"Watch them."

Then both men dropped to the ground and, whirling, fired. Harlan felt lead nick his coat, and then he fired at the flash of the gun on his left. He was conscious of the fact that Bannion had gone down without even firing his gun.

The man Harlan had fired at was down, but the second man leaped to his feet and started down the hill at top speed. Harlan picked him off coolly in the dim light, dropping him at a distance of about twenty yards.

He went over to Dave Bannion, who was rolling on the ground, cursing, holding his upper right leg.

"Got me in the leg," he growled. "I figured they had guns on them, Harlan. See you got both of 'em."

"I'll be back," Harlan said. "I'll run a buckboard up here to take you down."

"Ain't no rush," Bannion muttered morosely. "I'm not goin' anywhere now."

Harlan had a look at the first man he'd hit, and found him still alive, although with a bullet through his chest. The second man was dead, shot through the back as he ran. He'd probably died before his body had even hit the ground. He knew neither man, which meant nothing.

The wounded man was mumbling something, his head rolling from side to side.

"Get you into town," Harlan told him. "See what we can do for you. You don't deserve much, though."

Untying his horse, Harlan rode down into town and located Cole McAfee out in front of the Cheyenne Saloon. They procured a buckboard from the nearest livery stable and rode up the hill, Harlan giving McAfee the details of the fight as they went up the grade.

"Bannion's not hurt bad?" McAfee asked.

"Shot through the leg," Harlan told him. "Can't tell how bad it is."

"Other fellow's alive?"

"Was alive when I left him," Harlan said. "He had it in the chest."

"He might talk," McAfee observed. "He might tell who sent him. Then we got something to work on."

They found Dave Bannion sitting up, still muttering to himself, and McAfee said to him, "Think it hit a bone, Dave?"

"I don't figure it's too bad," Bannion growled. "Just mad that I didn't give it to them dogs when I had the chance."

"Harlan got them," McAfee said. "Let's see if we can get you into this buckboard, Dave."

They lifted the wounded man up into the buckboard, placing him upon a pile of blankets McAfee had thoughtfully tossed into the wagon, and then went to have a look at the other man.

He was still alive, though unconscious. McAfee said, "We'll get him down to Doc Holsworth. He might talk there."

They lifted the wounded man into the wagon beside Dave Bannion, and rode back to town. Boyd Garrison and Fred Barnhouse met them coming down the hill; both of them had heard of the fight.

Harlan gave them the story as they rode beside the buckboard back into town. When he'd finished Barnhouse said:

"What'll you do if this fellow tells you he was hired by Andrews?"

"We're taking Andrews in," Harlan told him, "according to McAfee here."

"That right?" Barnhouse murmured.

"You heard him right," McAfee growled.

"You forgetting about the Lester brothers?" Barnhouse asked him. "You'll have to walk past them to get at Mr. Andrews, you know."

"Then we'll walk past them," McAfee said stubbornly.

Boyd Garrison had been silent on the ride down the hill. As they were pulling up in front of the doctor's house at the far end of town he said to Harlan:

"They didn't do much damage to the High Dollar. The attack was a diversion to destroy by Big Bonanza shafthouse again."

"Figured that," Harlan said.

They carried Dave Bannion into the house, and then came back for the wounded man still in the buckboard. He was conscious now, and mumbling to himself.

Doc Holsworth, a small, dapper man with a short beard, had one look at him, and said briefly, "He might live till morning, not any longer."

The wounded man heard the remark, and his eyes fluttered. He stared up at the ceiling, fear coming over his face.

"Can you talk?" McAfee asked him as the physician went to work on Bannion's leg in another room.

The man on the cot nodded. His face was ashen, and he was beginning to tremble.

"What's your name?" McAfee asked him.

Boyd Garrison and Fred Barnhouse were in the room with Harlan, and all were listening.

"Keefe," the man on the cot whispered. "Ed Keefe."

"Who sent you to dynamite the Big Bonanza shafthouse?" McAfee asked him. "Who paid you the money?"

"Jack Powers," Keefe told him in a low voice. "Am I finished, mister?"

"We'll have the doc work on you soon as he gets the bullet out of my deputy," McAfee assured him. "So Powers hired you."

Fred Barnhouse said to Harlan, "Powers is Andrews' man at the Bengal Tiger. He took over Griff Morgan's job."

"So it was Andrews," Garrison said softly.

"You'll sign a statement," McAfee said to the dying man, "that Powers paid you to wreck that shafthouse."

"Ain't signin' no statement," Keefe muttered. "Powers will kill me."

"You don't sign a statement," McAfee snapped, "and you'll lie here and bleed to death. I won't let the doc work on you."

Keefe coughed, and blood came to his lips. He was bleeding inwardly, although the chest wound showed very little blood.

"I'll sign it," he murmured.

McAfee looked at Harlan, and both of them knew that the issue was resolved right there. It had finally come to a head. They did not have Andrews, but they had his man, his hired employee, who had paid a drifter to wreck the installations of a rival mine operator.

They would have to arrest Jack Powers, and in doing so they would come in open conflict with the Lesters, which meant a fight. Andrews could not afford to let them jail Powers and get a confession out of him that he'd been taking orders from Andrews.

Barnhouse brought out a piece of paper, and McAfee wrote a statement on it. He helped prop Jack Keefe up on the cot, and the wounded man signed the statement, which was duly witnessed by Harlan and Garrison.

CHAPTER
FIFTEEN

Harlan walked back to the Empire Hotel with Garrison and Fred Barnhouse; Cole McAfee had arranged to meet him there later. McAfee had promised Keefe that he'd communicate with his brother up in Saddletop, and was now writing a note for the dying man.

On the way to the hotel Harlan said to Garrison, "How is Julia taking it now?"

"Better than I thought she would," Garrison told him. "Marcia Reynolds is with her."

"What are her plans?" Harlan wanted to know.

"Quite early to say what she'll do," Garrison told him. "She has an aunt in Indiana. Other than that I know of no relatives."

"Girl that age should be getting married," Barnhouse observed.

Boyd Garrison said nothing to that, and Harlan wondered at his silence. When Barnhouse left them in front of the hotel, Harlan asked bluntly, "You going to marry Julia Brynn?"

Boyd Garrison turned to look at him quizzically. "I don't know, Harlan," he admitted.

"You want to marry her?"

"I'm not sure of that, either," Garrison confessed. He added thoughtfully, "You interested, Harlan?"

"I might be," Harlan told him.

"Then don't let me stand in your way."

"I don't have what you have to offer." Harlan smiled faintly.

"That won't make any difference to Julia Brynn," Garrison assured him. "Believe me on that score, Harlan."

Harlan didn't say anything to that. He sat down on the porch of the Empire Hotel and he waited for Cole McAfee to come.

Boyd Garrison walked away from him and stood at the end of the porch. While he was standing there Cole McAfee came up, and Harlan tossed away his cigar and stood up.

McAfee paused below him on the other side of the railing. He said quietly, "Reckon we have some work to do, Craig. You ready?"

"Ready," Harlan said, and he went down to the walk. He felt for the gun under his coat, loosening it in the holster.

They walked past Boyd Garrison without a word, and he watched them go. McAfee said:

"We're picking up Jack Powers, and I expect the Lesters to try to stop us if they get wind of it. The chances are that Mr. Andrews has already learned we've caught his man Keefe, and that Keefe has probably talked. He'll know then that we're after Powers, and he'll pass the word to the Lester brothers that the time has come. You afraid to die, Craig?"

"No," Harlan said. "I'd rather live, though."

"You may die tonight," McAfee told him calmly. "You know how fast these boys are with six-guns."

"A chance I took when I asked for this job," Harlan replied. "I'm with it."

They entered the crowded Montana Saloon, and McAfee pushed his way up to the bar. He said to the bartender:

"Jack Powers been in here?"

"Not tonight," the bartender told him.

Men nearby looked at them as they turned to go out. One man said jocularly, "You got trouble, Marshal?"

"We take it where we go," McAfee told him.

They moved on to another saloon, doing it methodically, without haste, because there was plenty of time. When they'd been in a half-dozen saloons without catching up with their man, Harlan said thoughtfully:

"You figure Powers got his orders to clear out of Rimrock until this thing was settled?"

McAfee grimaced. "Could be," he admitted, "but I'm figuring we'll still have the Lesters to deal with. They won't run, and Andrews brought them here to throw their weight around."

By the time they'd covered one side of the street, the news had gone out that they were looking for a man. They were watched furtively as they crossed the road and started down the other side. They had seen neither Jack Powers nor the two Lester brothers.

A bartender in the Alhambra Bar, however, informed them quietly that the Lesters were in the Cheyenne Saloon.

The Cheyenne was a few doors down the street, and there were several saloons they still had to enter, but already Harlan could feel tension building up inside of him.

They entered the Stallion Saloon, and then the Cheyenne, and the Cheyenne was almost empty. Three men stood at the bar. The two Lester brothers stood on either side of a gaunt, hatchet-faced man in black with a string tie. The gaunt man had an insolent grin on his face. He wore a gun strapped around his waist, and his coat was open, giving him easy access to the gun.

There were no bartenders behind the bar, all of them having left. A few men stood along the far walls, but when McAfee and Harlan came in they left by a side door.

"Man in the middle," McAfee said, "is Powers."

John Lester, with the mustache, stood to the right of Powers, and Trev Lester to the left. When the two lawmen came in they moved a little farther away from Powers so that now nearly two yards separated the three men.

The Lester brothers watched like two cats, unsmiling, their dull green eyes glowing. Trev Lester had both elbows back on the bar wood, his right hand hanging near the gun on his right hip. John Lester stood away from the bar, as indolent as a cat, completely relaxed, but ready to spring into action.

Cole McAfee said, "Come to take you in, Powers."

Powers grinned. "What for?"

"Have a paper in my pocket," McAfee told him patiently, "says you paid a man named Keefe and others to dynamite the Big Bonanza shafthouse. Keefe signed the paper, and it was witnessed. It's legal in any court of the land."

"Didn't know we had a court in Rimrock." Powers chuckled. "Ain't no use arresting me, McAfee."

"Taking you in," McAfee repeated. "You want to throw down that gunbelt?"

"No judge on the bench to try me." Powers laughed. "Why arrest a man you can't try, McAfee? Wait'll we get a judge in this town."

"I don't wait," McAfee said, and Harlan noticed that he moved away slightly to his right, putting more space between them.

John Lester said thoughtfully, "Reckon he's a man in a hurry. Where you hurrying to, Marshal?"

"Boot Hill," his brother answered for him. "He's hurrying to Boot Hill."

"Take both you boys with me," McAfee said. "Stay out of this."

"We're in it," Trev Lester said easily. "Let's get it straight from the start."

McAfee said again, "You coming out, Powers?"

Jack Powers shook his head slowly. "Have to go feet first if I go," he said. "That's how it is, Marshal."

Behind him Harlan heard the bat-wing doors swing gently, and he saw Powers and the two Lesters stare curiously at someone who'd come in behind them.

Boyd Garrison said gently, "Will you deputize me, McAfee, right now?"

Harlan didn't turn his head to look, but he was conscious of the fact that Garrison had come in between McAfee and himself, and was standing there calmly.

"You're crazy," McAfee muttered.

"I started this fight," Garrison said quietly. "Now I'm in it."

"You're not a gunfighter," Harlan told him, puzzled. "You couldn't hit a barn with a six-gun. They'll shoot you down."

"I can throw lead," Garrison told him, "until I'm shot down. I might even hit something. At any rate, I'll be a diversion. There are three of them, and they can't wholly forget about me."

Neither Harlan nor McAfee said anything for a moment, and then McAfee said slowly:

"You're a millionaire, Garrison. You could hire men to do this work for you."

"I had to fight for my money," Boyd Garrison told him, "for every penny of it, but never like this. It won't hurt me to fight like this, too, if other men have to do it."

"Just talk around here," John Lester murmured. "I don't like talk. All I hear is talk."

"Use your gun, then," Harlan invited.

John Lester said, "Here it is," and he drew his gun.

Harlan had seen men draw guns before, but never like this. John Lester had been completely relaxed, and even in this position his gun hand moved with lightning speed. The gun barrel was coming up toward Harlan even as his own gun was still in the holster, not completely out.

He heard Cole McAfee yell a warning, and he was aware of the fact that Trev Lester and Powers were also going for their guns. But he kept his eyes on brother John, and he did a very unusual thing.

Instead of remaining where he was, or trying to dodge from John Lester's lead, he moved straight forward at his man, firing as he advanced, and it was this movement, wholly unorthodox, which saved his life.

John Lester did not expect him to come forward, straight at him, and the maneuver confused him. His first shot, which should have killed Harlan at close range, only grazed his left arm at the elbow.

Harlan's shot smashed the top button on John Lester's vest, knocking him back against the bar, a stunned, bewildered expression on his face, his gun drooping in his hand.

Harlan wasted no more time on him. The Cheyenne Saloon was booming with sound, four other guns roaring at the same time. At a distance of less than eight feet, Harlan turned his gun on Jack Powers and fired twice.

The tall, gaunt United Copper man was backed against the bar, cringing a little, but turning his fire on Boyd Garrison. Harlan's two shots dropped him into the sawdust, which left only Trev Lester on his feet. But Trev had been hit, too.

He was swaying a little, his eyes glassy, licking his lips with his tongue, just before he fell.

Cole McAfee was down, too, sprawled on his face, head toward the bar, the gun dropped from his hand.

Boyd Garrison, strangely enough, was still standing along with Harlan, the only other man of the six on his feet. Garrison had been hit in the left arm. He held his arm with his free hand, and Harlan saw blood dripping to the floor from his fingertips.

Trev Lester's body hit the sawdust with a sickening thud, the way a dead man falls. He didn't move after he fell. He lay there with his arms outstretched, his toes pointing inward, and a pool of blood started to form underneath him as his life's blood flowed out.

Jack Powers had fallen back against the bar and was sitting there, his hands at his sides, jaw drooping, dullness in his eyes.

Harlan hurried over to Cole McAfee, giving Garrison a quick look as he went by. He rolled the marshal over, and saw the stain of blood on his shirt front, low down on the left side.

"Got me twice," McAfee muttered, "before I hit him once. He was greased lightning, like they said."

"You got him," Harlan said. "Where's the other wound?"

"Leg," McAfee gasped. "Right leg above the knee. That's what knocked me down."

Garrison came over, his face pale. He said, "Can I do anything, Harlan?"

"You all right?" Harlan asked him.

"Just a flesh wound in the arm," Garrison murmured. "I'm more scared than anything else. I'm still not sure what happened. I know I fired a few shots, and then they were all down."

"You missed." Harlan smiled. "Tell someone outside to bring up Doc Holsworth."

Garrison walked to the door, where the crowd was peering in now that the shooting had stopped. He sent a runner off for the physician, and then he came back to where Harlan was half-dragging, half-carrying McAfee to a back room where a bartender had informed him there was a cot.

"My first gun fight," Garrison murmured, "and my last." He nodded toward the three men on the floor. "Dead?"

"They're dead," Harlan told him.

"Quick," Garrison murmured. "A matter of seconds. I didn't think people could die that quickly."

"They do," Harlan assured him.

They put McAfee up on the cot, and he cut away the pants leg to reveal the leg wound.

"Looks like it missed the bone," Harlan said. "You're lucky, McAfee."

"Other one must have knocked out a rib or two," McAfee scowled. "You talk about luck, coming through a fight like that without a scratch."

"I don't know how John Lester missed me," Harlan said. "I must be made for better things."

Doc Holsworth came in with his bag, shaking his head grimly. "Bashed heads and bullet wounds," he said. "What a town!"

"It'll be better from now on," Boyd Garrison assured him. He sat on a chair on the other side of the room, still holding his wounded arm, waiting for the physician to look at McAfee first.

"How will it be better?" Harlan asked him.

"I'm selling out to Mr. Andrews," Garrison told him. "I'm through in Rimrock. I've caused enough trouble here."

McAfee said from the cot, "Smartest thing you ever did, Garrison. You're fixed with money, and we'll have a little peace in this town. Andrews is a crook, but he'll keep the mines open and there'll be no more fighting."

"Andrews won't live six months," Doc Holsworth said quietly as he looked at the wound in McAfee's side.

"How's that?" the marshal asked him.

"He's a sick man," the doctor told him. "Kidneys are shot. I give him six months with luck."

"Then I might come back here some day as an honest mine operator," Garrison said thoughtfully, "but I'm getting out now, in the morning. It's best for now."

"Never expected you to walk into the Cheyenne Saloon like that," Harlan said. "You surprised me, Garrison."

"I am not a coward," Garrison stated.

"We'll vouch for that," McAfee said.

After both McAfee and Garrison had been treated, and Harlan had helped get McAfee back to his quarters at the boardinghouse, and into bed, he retired himself. It was past three in the morning now, but the town was strangely quiet. It was as if the epic fight inside the Cheyenne Saloon had sobered men. The rumor had gone through town, also, that the mines were reopening in the morning, and this had had its effect on the miners.

166

When Harlan finally retired to his own room he was completely exhausted. It was high noon before he awoke.

He hurried to McAfee's room to find him awake and with a slight fever, which Doc Holsworth had said might come, but otherwise in good shape. A woman had stayed with him during the night to see if he needed anything, but she left the room for a few minutes when Harlan came in.

"We have a clean town," McAfee said. "Reckon you're the only one of us left to keep it that way, Harlan, until I get back on my feet." He looked at Harlan curiously. "What's for you in this town?"

Harlan shrugged. "Reckon I take one thing at a time," he said. "I wanted to see this through."

"You won't stay on as my deputy any more than you stayed on as Garrison's bodyguard."

"No," Harlan said. "I'll see what turns up."

"Hope it's good." McAfee smiled. "You rate it."

Harlan went out into the street, and he looked up the hill in the direction of the Big Bonanza Mine. He could see the piles of clean timber there, but no workmen in the vicinity. Ore cars were rolling from the High Dollar, though, and when he looked in the direction of the Bengal Tiger Mine he could see the cars sliding down the little railways.

He turned in the direction of the Empire Hotel, and met Fred Barnhouse coming from his newspaper office. Barnhouse's thin face was expressionless. He said briefly:

"Big news today is that Boyd Garrison sold his interests in this town to William Andrews, and left on the eastboard train thirty minutes ago."

"He's gone!" Harlan gasped.

"Wanted to move quickly," Barnhouse told him. "I understand he left with a woman."

Slowly Harlan walked on to the Empire Hotel, his mind in a whirl. Had Garrison gone with Julia Brynn?

Harlan was feeling a little sick when he stepped into the lobby of the Empire Hotel. In a moment he would learn if Julia was gone.

The hotel clerk said immediately when he came in, "Letter for you, Mr. Craig, from Mr. Garrison."

The letter was not long, and it was more than Harlan had expected.

"I regret that I must leave you without saying goodbye, Harlan," Garrison had written, "but were I to remain and try to convince you of the logic of my offer, your pride would interfere, and you would feel that I were giving you a handout. My proposition is far from that. I need a man of your calibre, and if I do not make the offer to you I will have to make it to another man whom I do not know, and whom I cannot trust."

The proposition surprised Harlan, also. One of Boyd Garrison's wide-flung enterprises was a narrow gauge line running from Saddletop up to Middleview, another mining town, and then through the mountains to the coast. Garrison was positive the line would be needed, and that it would be a moneymaker. He'd just begun to lay track, and he needed a man to set the line up and sell it to the public. Garrison judged that Harlan was

168

the man to do that, and he was offering him a half-interest in the railroad if he would take it over now that Garrison was being forced to leave the scene.

"I am leaving Rimrock with the woman I love," Garrison finished his letter. "Write me in Chicago if you are willing to accept my proposition. Whatever you do, luck and prosperity to you."

Harlan folded the letter. Garrison's proposition was a good one, exactly the kind of thing he wanted. He'd had experience with a stage line, and he thought he could run a small railroad without too much trouble, and perhaps build it into something bigger as the years went on. At least it was a beginning, and Garrison did need someone to handle it for him.

There was still the matter of the "woman I love." Garrison stared at the letter. The woman could be either Julia Brynn or Marcia Reynolds.

The clerk was still behind the desk, filing letters, and Harlan cleared his throat before asking him if Julia Brynn were still registered at the hotel. Then he heard steps on the stairs, and when he looked up he saw Julia coming down.

Her face was pale but composed, and she smiled at him as he stood up, hat in hand.

"You didn't leave," he said.

"No," she told him. "Mr. Garrison left this morning with Miss Reynolds. I believe he intends to marry her."

Harlan stood there, twisting his hat in his hands. "Glad for them," he said. "I wanted to know."

"I'm glad for them, too," Julia Brynn told him.

"You're not disappointed?" Harlan murmured.

She looked at him steadily. "No," she said.

"Can I take you to dinner?" Harlan asked her.

"It would be a great pleasure." Julia Brynn smiled, and took his arm, and as they walked toward the hotel dining room he felt the pressure of her fingers on his arm, and he looked down at her, and saw that she was smiling. He knew that this was the way it would be with them, always.